"You'd be quite willing to let me seduce you, I suppose."

"Come on, Janey. If that kiss wasn't an invitation—"

"I was not kissing you!" Her voice was fierce and Maddy jerked in surprise and wailed. Janey scooped the baby up into her arms, and Maddy relaxed again, her face nestled against Janey's breast.

"I assure you," Webb said cheerfully, "I do know a kiss when I—"

"I want you to understand I'm not interested in you personally. My only goal is the money you promised me!"

"Want to place a little bet? That it won't be the last suggestive kiss you'll ever give me?"

The Tycoon's Baby
Leigh Michaels

HARLEQUIN®

TORONTO • NEW YORK • LONDON
AMSTERDAM • PARIS • SYDNEY • HAMBURG
STOCKHOLM • ATHENS • TOKYO • MILAN • MADRID
PRAGUE • WARSAW • BUDAPEST • AUCKLAND

ISBN 0-373-03574-8

THE TYCOON'S BABY

First North American Publication 1999.

Copyright © 1999 by Leigh Michaels.

Visit us at www.romance.net

Printed in U.S.A.

CHAPTER ONE

THE room rang with the sound of a toddler's giggles. Webb raised himself up on one elbow and leaned over the pajama-clad child who was sprawled on the Oriental rug in front of the fireplace. He growled gently as he threatened once more to gobble her tummy, and she shrieked with delight and yanked his hair.

Nearby, a white-uniformed woman shifted to the edge of her chair and said, "Mr. Copeland, it's Madeline's bedtime."

Who cares? Webb wanted to say. *I don't, and Madeline certainly doesn't.* "I've only seen my little girl for twenty minutes all day, Mrs. Wilson. Can't her bedtime be put off for a while?"

The nurse's expression was stern. "I'd say you've already managed that. You've got her so agitated it'll take an hour just to get her settled."

Webb sighed and made a vow to himself that tomorrow he *would* get out of the office on time, no matter what. "All right." He bent over the toddler again. "Maddy, playtime's over. Give me a kiss before you go up to bed."

Madeline's enormous brown eyes—her mother's eyes—pleaded silently, but Webb gathered her close and stood up. He rubbed his cheek against her soft dark hair and kissed her rosy cheek, then handed her over to the nurse and watched the pair of them cross the marble-tiled foyer and climb the winding stairs.

The tiny woman perched on a low rocking chair at one side of the fireplace didn't look up from the mass of rose-colored yarn in her lap. The flicker of the flames cast long shadows, which emphasized the deep lines etched in her face. "I don't know why you put up with that woman, Webb."

"Because she's the best baby nurse in Cook County."

Camilla Copeland sniffed. "Says who?"

"She was highly recommended."

"She's rigid."

"Gran, you can't have it both ways. I've heard you say yourself that children need schedules."

"I said they need security and stability. That does not mean I'm in favor of regimentation."

Webb buttoned the collar of his pin-striped shirt and settled his tie back into place. "Gran, please don't start this again." But he might as well have tried to stop a battleship.

"Madeline's only fifteen months old. Don't you think it's a bit early for her to be living a boarding school lifestyle, all bells and whistles and rules?" Camilla Copeland looked straight at her grandson and added firmly, "The child needs a mother."

Webb dropped into a chair. He might as well make himself as comfortable as possible. They'd had this discussion a dozen times at least, and he knew better than to think he could cut it short now, because, once launched, Camilla was inexorable.

Her voice softened. "I know it affected you horribly, when Sibyl…went—"

"You have no idea, Gran."

"But it's been more than a year since she died, and it's time for you to get on with your life."

"I *am* getting on with my life. What I don't plan to do is get married again—ever."

"Oh, my dear." Camilla's voice was soft. "I know that you've been stunned—almost in a daze—ever since the accident. But you mustn't assume that because you haven't felt any interest in women in this past year that you never will. Those…urges…aren't gone, Webb.''

Despite his annoyance with her, Webb had to bite back a laugh. Dear old Gran, with her Victorian way of putting things! She'd even turned just a little pink, bless her heart. Or was that simply the firelight reflecting off the half-finished sweater in her lap?

Camilla turned her knitting and started another row. ''Someday, Webb, I promise you'll be eager to have a woman in your life again.''

Webb wondered what she'd say if he pointed out that he'd only ruled out marriage, not the possibility of another woman in his life.

''And it'll be easier for Madeline to accept a stepmother now than it will be later.'' Camilla nodded firmly, as if she'd nailed her point and was assured there could be no argument.

Webb blinked in surprise. He'd thought he could practically recite this entire conversation from beginning to end with all its variations, but that last line had been a completely new twist. He felt like a skier who'd wandered off the marked trail and found himself speeding down the side of an entirely different mountain.

''Now wait a minute,'' he said. ''Because you're so certain that someday I'll decide to get married again, you think I should leap into it right now—whether I'm ready or not—because Maddy's the right age to bond with a stepmother?''

''I didn't say you should leap,'' Camilla said. ''I said you shouldn't write off the possibility.''

Webb shook his head. ''No, you weren't nearly that flexible, Gran. So let's assume I take your advice and get married, against my better judgment, purely so Maddy can have a stepmother—''

"I never indicated that you should consider only what's best for Madeline. I expect you'd have a few criteria of your own."

"That's very generous of you," Webb said with mock humility. "I'm grateful to have a say in this."

"Don't be impudent, Webb." Camilla pushed her knitting needles deep into the mass of pink yarn. "There's the bell, and we won't be able to finish this discussion over dinner."

Because the butler would hear, Webb thought. *Thank heaven for small blessings.*

"But I want your promise that you'll think it over."

Webb offered his arm. "I assure you, Gran," he said gravely, "that I'll give the idea all the consideration it deserves."

Camilla's eyes narrowed, but she didn't leap on the irony in his voice. "And we'll talk about this again."

That, Webb thought, *is precisely what I'm afraid of.*

As the clock neared three, the mood of the students in the lecture hall shifted from attentive to restless. Papers shuffled, notebooks closed, books scraped as they were loaded into backpacks. Finally, in the middle of a sentence, the professor seemed to notice the time. "Test next Monday," he reminded, "after the Thanksgiving break." The rush to the door began.

Janey Griffin stayed in her seat at the back corner of the room, finishing up her notes and waiting for the traffic jam to clear. In a couple of minutes, she'd be able to walk straight through the building without having to dodge the crowds. Besides, she needed to finish writing down the professor's last line of logic before she left the room, because she'd never be able to reconstruct it tonight after work.

Outside the classroom, a petite blonde was waiting for

her, leaning against the wall with her books folded in her arms. She fell into step beside Janey. "Do you have time for a cup of coffee?"

Janey shook her head. "I'm due at work in an hour. You can walk over to the apartment with me if you like, and talk while I change clothes. What is it, Ellen? Boyfriend problems again?"

"Dennis is being a jerk." Ellen sounded almost absent-minded. "But that's nothing new. I can't believe you've still got this job."

"Why? I'm a good worker. In another month, I'll be finished with my probation, and I'll even get a raise—"

"And another noisy, greasy, disgusting machine to run."

"Somebody has to make drive shafts, honey, or your little red car would be a paperweight instead of transportation." Janey dodged traffic to cross the street, which separated the campus from a residential area.

Ellen broke into a run to catch up. "But why does it have to be you? If you soak your hands for a year, you'll never get all the grease out of your skin. I can't believe you haven't quit by now."

"It's good money, and the hours are compatible with the classes I need to take. Besides, what would I do instead? Wait tables? Sorry, dear, but I'd rather smell of machine oil than french-fry grease. To say nothing of dealing with obnoxious customers…"

Which wouldn't be any easier than dealing with the jerks on the manufacturing line, she reminded herself.

Ellen seemed to have read her mind. "Are the men still harassing you?"

"Now and then," Janey admitted. She pulled out her keys as she ducked down the stairs beside a run-down old house to her apartment in the basement.

"What does that mean? Is it a constant hassle, or do they

let you take breaks from it once in a while?'' Ellen shook her head. "And you still haven't reported them?''

"What good would it do? I'd just get myself labeled a troublemaker, which is hardly what I want before I'm even through my trial employment period. The things they do are never so clearly abusive that it's obvious, you know, or the supervisors would have seen it already.''

"So go over their heads.''

"Oh, right. I'll just march into Webb Copeland's office and announce that he has a bunch of sexist redneck jerks working on the manufacturing line. And I'm sure he'll promote me to corporate vice president and put me in charge of sensitivity training.''

She pushed the door open. The apartment looked worse than usual, with her roommate's clothes and belongings strewn across the living-room furniture.

Ellen looked around. "Has Kasey been hosting police raids? It looks like someone's been executing a search warrant in here.''

Janey smiled. "Actually it's an improvement over the upholstery. Kasey has better taste in clothes than the landlord does in furniture.''

Ellen's face was tight. "You have a horrible job, you study the most incredible hours, you live in a rat hole...''

"Ellen, please—''

"I just hate it that you have to work so hard for this!'' Tears gleamed in Ellen's eyes, and her fists clenched.

Janey said lightly, "Oh, it's good for my soul to work hard. Besides, it's what I get for not starting college on time. Since I had a job those few years in between and I actually made a little money, I can't get any real financial help now.'' She unearthed a box of tissues buried under a pile of Kasey's sweaters and handed it to Ellen.

Absently Ellen pulled a tissue from the box. "Maybe my father could loan you some money."

"Don't you dare ask him," Janey ordered. "Even if he had the spare cash, it wouldn't be fair to put him on the spot. Anyway, I won't ask anybody to loan me money unless I can come up with something to offer as security—and that's about as likely as being struck by lightning. Look, Ellen, I know you only bring it up because you care. But being reminded of my circumstances doesn't change them, it just encourages me to feel sorry for myself."

Ellen sniffed and blew her nose. "I have never known you to feel sorry for yourself."

Janey smiled. "I'm glad to find out it doesn't show." She went into her tiny bedroom to change into the faded jeans and shabby flannel shirt she wore to work.

She wiped off her makeup, since in the factory's heat it would slide off her face anyway, and pulled her hair into a tight braid, which would keep it out of reach of the machines she'd be running—and tried to put what Ellen had said out of her mind.

It wasn't as if anyone was holding a gun to her head, forcing her to live this way, Janey reminded herself. She'd chosen to sacrifice her living standard and to work at a job she didn't like because her long-term goals were more important.

In another couple of years, she'd be far enough along in her education to qualify for internships in her field, and she'd be able to build experience and develop contacts that would help in her eventual search for a full-time job. But most internships didn't pay, and even if she was lucky enough to land one of the few that did, she couldn't make enough money to support herself and finish her last year of school, too.

So in the meantime she needed to put away all the money

she could—and that meant for the next two years she'd be working the swing shift at Copeland Products.

Two more years of running noisy, messy machines, carving and bending solid metal into vehicle parts. Two more years of fellow employees who were unused to working side by side with women on the production line, men who vented their discomfort in crude remarks. Two more years of coming home after midnight exhausted and filthy, to be greeted by a stack of homework and an alarm clock already ticking ominously toward a too-early morning.

Two more years. It sounded like eternity.

Janey took a deep breath and forced herself to smile. She'd take it one day at a time, and she'd pull through...because she had to.

The Copeland Products factory was brilliantly lit and incredibly noisy, for even during the change of shifts the machines kept running. As Janey crossed the factory floor to check in with her supervisor, her safety goggles were still dangling on their strap around her neck, but she made sure her electronic earmuffs were already in place. The earmuffs were less than comfortable, but the up-to-date engineering muted the roar of the machinery while allowing the human voice to come through loud and strong. Janey wasn't so sure that was really a technological advance; given her choice, she'd have opted for cotton balls instead so she wouldn't have to listen to her fellow workers. Certain ones of them, at any rate.

She arrived at her assigned post with a minute to spare, and the man who'd operated the machine on the day shift stepped aside. "It's been running a little wild," he said. "I've been adjusting it all day, but it keeps throwing the shavings instead of dropping them into the bin. I'm starting to think we've got a bad batch of steel and it's not the machine at all.''

''Great,'' Janey muttered, and watched intently as he showed her the adjustments he'd made. As soon as he left she pulled up a tall stool so she could perch high enough to keep an eye on every moving part. If she was going to have to baby-sit the machine, she might as well be comfortable.

The man at the next machine called, ''Wish I could sit down on the job.''

She looked over in surprise. The man who usually ran that piece of equipment—the one who so frequently entertained himself by tossing suggestive remarks at Janey—was nowhere to be seen, and this worker was obviously settling in for the shift.

The wave of relief that surged over Janey surprised her just a little. She hadn't realized how tightly controlled she'd been until suddenly she was free of the need to guard herself at every moment.

Enjoy it while it lasts, she told herself. *He'll probably be back tomorrow.*

Despite the warnings, the machine seemed to be on its best behavior through the first half of the shift. As her hands automatically moved pieces from the supply pile to the machine to the pallet full of processed metal ready to move on to the next step, Janey's brain was reviewing that last lecture and thinking ahead to next week's test.

It was almost time for her midshift break when the machine began to groan and rattle as the day worker had warned it might, and she slowed it to a crawl and reached for the tool kit.

She had just opened the safety guard to make the necessary adjustments when the substitute worker next to her suggested that the two of them coordinate their break time so they could spend a few minutes in the back seat of his car—and he didn't hesitate to describe the activity he had in mind.

Janey was so taken aback that she turned to stare at him, and in the instant her attention was distracted the cutting blade caught and jerked and flung a red-hot fragment. It hit the unprotected skin on the side of her neck, and she heard the sizzle even before she felt the heat.

She dropped the safety guard shut and cupped a gloved hand over the wound, wincing as the pain surged in waves like an incoming tide.

Within a minute the supervisor was beside her. "Dammit, Griffin," he said, "we were working our way up to a perfect injury-free month, and now you do this."

The man at the next machine said virtuously, "It's a good thing I asked you about your family just then, Griffin. If you hadn't turned your head you'd have gotten that piece of steel right in the face."

Between the pain and his bold-faced lie, Janey was too stunned even to speak.

"That's about the way it looks to me," the supervisor said. "What were you thinking of to open the safety guard, anyway?"

From behind Janey came another voice—rich and deep, with a note which almost sounded like kindness. "Gentlemen, let's treat the injury before we dissect the accident."

Slowly, as if she were a music box figurine with no say in her own movements, Janey turned to face the man who'd spoken.

She'd seen Webb Copeland before, of course; he frequently walked the production lines, though not usually at this hour of the evening. But she'd never been this close to him before.

He was taller than she'd thought. Or perhaps it was the

charcoal trench coat he wore, open over a pin-striped gray suit, which emphasized both his height and the width of his shoulders.

His eyes, she noted, were the same silvery gray as the steel she handled every day, though they didn't look as chilly. His dark brows were drawn together, giving his entire face an expression of concern that was even more appealing than his good looks.

And then Janey noticed something really odd. The smell of oil in the factory was so strong that she'd never been aware of any other scent before. But now from four feet away she could breathe the essence of Webb Copeland's cologne. In fact, the aroma made her feel just a little dizzy...

His eyes narrowed. "You're going to the infirmary right now to get that burn looked at. In fact, I'll take you down."

Janey's feminist streak wanted to say, *I'll go to the infirmary when and if I darned well please, and I don't need to be delivered there like a package.* But common sense interceded and she obediently walked beside him across the factory floor to the door that led to the office wing.

As the roar of the factory faded, Janey realized she was still wearing her electronic earmuffs, and she snatched them off. The office wing stretched before them, its silence almost more deafening than the roar of the machines.

She broke it hesitantly. "I don't even know where the infirmary is."

"If that's your way of telling me you're not in the habit of injuring yourself on the job, don't worry," he said with a trace of humor. "If you were, I'd have heard about it by now."

"That's not...I just meant I've only been in the office wing once, and that was the day I was hired."

"When was that?"

Janey said reluctantly, "Two months ago." She wondered if he was thinking, as she was, that there was still another month to go before the company would decide if she was an employee they wanted to keep or more trouble than she was worth.

Great move, Janey, she told herself. *You don't only break the safety record, but you do it right in front of the boss. And then you point out how inexperienced you are.*

A middle-aged woman in a long white lab coat stepped out of a room at the end of a hallway. "The supervisor called to tell me you were on the way," she said. "Let me take a look." She inspected the side of Janey's neck and shook her head. "Second degree burn—bad enough, but it's not large and not particularly deep. It'll hurt like fury for a while, and you'll probably have a very interesting scar. Come on in. Let's get it clean so we can see about minimizing the damage."

The toe of Janey's steel-reinforced work shoe caught on the threshold of the treatment room, and she stumbled.

Webb Copeland caught her arm and steadied her. "Those things aren't much like ballet slippers, are they?"

"Not unless ballet slippers weigh half a ton apiece." She glanced around the room and decided to sit in a chair rather than climb onto the examining table. "I wouldn't know, because I never took dance lessons."

He said evenly, "Of course not. I beg your pardon."

Embarrassed at her sharpness, Janey rubbed her temple. "Sorry to snap at you. Look, I didn't intend to come off like a clinging vine just now. I don't make a habit of tripping over thin air and expecting the nearest man to catch me. I jog. I lift weights." *At least I used to, when I had time,* she thought. "I even changed the oil in my car when I had one. So if you're harboring any doubts about whether I really can run that machine, Mr. Copeland—"

He leaned against a rank of stainless steel cabinets. "I thought you'd get to the point eventually."

The nurse interrupted. "Hold still for a minute. This is only antibacterial soap, but it'll sting a bit."

And that was an understatement of the same magnitude as saying that Lake Michigan was damp, Janey thought. She tried to fight back the tears, but she wasn't entirely successful.

Webb Copeland opened a cabinet door and peered inside. If he was displaying tact by not watching her cry, Janey thought, she appreciated the gesture.

He started pushing bottles around. "Do you still keep antacids on hand, Nadine?"

So much for tact, Janey told herself. She should have expected he'd have an agenda of his own.

The nurse nodded. "Bottom shelf, on the left."

He found the bottle and dumped three tablets into his palm.

"Sorry to upset your stomach," Janey muttered.

He paused with the tablets halfway to his mouth. "When it comes to giving me heartburn, you can't begin to compete with my grandmother, Ms.... I don't seem to remember your name."

But of course after this you'll never forget it, Janey thought. She wanted to kick herself for drawing his attention once more. "Griffin." She could almost hear the click in his brain as he filed the information away.

He put the bottle back and leaned against the cabinet once more. "Now tell me what happened with that machine."

She described as clearly as she could what had gone wrong, and by the time she was done the nurse had finished treating the burn on her neck and covered it with a bandage to keep it clean.

Webb Copeland said nothing at all, just looked thoughtful.

The nurse counted out some painkillers into an envelope and handed it to Janey, and told her to stop by the infirmary again in a day or two to have the wound checked for infection.

Janey thanked her and gathered up her gloves and her electronic earmuffs. She had to force herself to stand up, and the thought of going back to work, of struggling once more with that machine, was hardly inviting. But she had a small burn, not a major disability—and the boss was watching.

Webb Copeland fell into step beside her in the hallway. Janey didn't look at him. "It was nice of you to stay," she said finally. "You didn't have to."

"I should thank *you*," he said. "I'd exhausted all my excuses for working late, and you provided me with a new one."

Janey frowned. Why should he need excuses for working late? In fact, why didn't he want to go home?

He followed her onto the factory floor. For a moment Janey wondered why, until she remembered that he'd been on his way out of the building when she'd been injured.

The supervisor was inspecting her machine. "That certainly took long enough," he said tartly as she approached. "What did they do? Skin grafts?" He didn't wait for an answer. "There doesn't appear to be anything wrong with the machinery. So unless you can give me a reason why I shouldn't put you on report for carelessness, Griffin—"

Janey thought about it, and shook her head. The lecher at the next machine had been the catalyst, but she *had* been careless, opening the guard like that and then allowing her mind to wander.

"Then get back to work," the supervisor ordered.

Behind her, Webb Copeland cleared his throat. "There will be no report of carelessness, because that machine is to be tagged as dangerous and taken out of production till we can get a repairman in to look at it. And since she has no equipment to work with, Ms. Griffin is not going back to work tonight, she is going home. Right now."

The supervisor's jaw dropped. The lecher at the next work station gasped.

Janey winced. But she could hardly stand in the middle of the factory and argue about it, so she meekly got her coat and keys from her locker in the break room and followed Webb Copeland out the employees' entrance. She stopped on the curb as the November wind cut through her coat.

"Did you say you don't have a car?" he asked.

"The bus will be along soon. Mr. Copeland, I wish you hadn't done that."

"Which part? And why not?"

"All of it—because there'll be a lot of talk."

"About what?"

"It's obvious you don't hang out with the guys on the factory floor, or you'd know." But it was cold, and her neck hurt, and he'd probably think she was conceited even to suggest that the workers were probably talking about the two of them right now. It was too late to do anything about it anyway. "Never mind," she muttered. "By the way, I hate to sound miserly, but is my paycheck going to be docked because I'm leaving early?"

"Since it's not your fault, no. Come on, I'll drive you home. It's silly to wait in the cold for a bus." He started off without even a look to see if she was coming along.

For some reason she'd pictured him in a low-slung, two-passenger convertible—but instead his car was midsized and quietly luxurious. "Of course," she muttered. "Grandma."

Webb slid behind the wheel. "I beg your pardon? I didn't quite catch that."

Janey was too embarrassed at being caught talking to herself even to duck the question. "I was just speculating that your grandmother would find it hard to get in and out of a Corvette."

He frowned. "You don't know my grandmother, do you?"

"Are you kidding? Of course I don't. What would I have in common with her?"

"An excellent question," he murmured. "Where do you live?"

She gave him the general direction and thought fleetingly about having him drop her off on campus instead of at her door. But why should it matter if Webb Copeland thought she lived in a slum?

It didn't, she told herself defiantly. Because *he* didn't matter. Not at all.

The engine purred as the car drew up next to one of the most bedraggled houses Webb had ever seen. He gave the place a glance and said, "I'll wait till you're inside."

Janey paused, half in and half out of the car. "Don't bother. I walk two blocks home from the bus stop every night, later than this, all by myself."

He waited nevertheless, watching intently till he saw a light come on in the basement apartment. Then he sat back and tapped his fingers on the leather-wrapped steering wheel, and indulged himself in a long, slow smile.

She's perfect, he told himself. *Utterly and absolutely perfect.*

*   *   *

The moment she walked into the employee break room the next day, Janey knew it was going to be worse than she'd thought possible. The looks were bad enough—sly sideways glances that slithered away like snakes when she tried to face them down. But as soon as she turned her back to get her safety equipment from her locker, the whispers started.

"Bet the big boss wouldn't have walked *me* to the infirmary."

"Or held your hand while the nasty nurse hurt you."

"Or taken you home afterward."

There was a snort of laughter. "I wonder if it was worth his while."

Janey had had enough. She turned to face them and said clearly, "If you mean, did Webb Copeland spend the night—no, he didn't."

One of the men leered. "Well, it probably wouldn't take all night," he said pointedly.

Janey flung her locker door shut and strode toward the factory entrance. Just outside the break room stood an elderly woman with half-glasses perched on her nose, holding a clipboard. She looked from it to Janey and asked, "Are you Ms. Griffin?"

"Unfortunately for me," Janey snapped, "yes."

The woman was unfazed. "Then if you'll come with me? I'm Mr. Copeland's private secretary, and he wishes to speak with you."

Janey stopped in midstep. "Is that so? Well, I've got a few things I wouldn't mind saying to him, too. Lead the way."

They wended down a different hall from the one which led to the infirmary. The farther they walked, Janey noticed, the grander the surroundings became. The carpets were deeper, the walls were papered or paneled instead of merely painted, and each office they passed was larger than the last.

And each person they met seemed increasingly startled at the sight of the two of them. Janey found some grim humor in that; the contrast between her—steel-toed shoes, safety goggles, electronic earmuffs and all—and the elegantly-turned-out white-haired secretary must be a stunner.

At the end of the building, as far as it was possible to get from the factory floor, the secretary opened a heavy teak door and said, "Mr. Copeland? Ms. Griffin is here."

Janey took two steps forward into an enormous office and watched as Webb Copeland rose slowly from behind an enormous desk.

Irrationally she found herself thinking that it hadn't been the trench coat that had made him look so tall last night. He really was as imposing as he'd seemed.

"Have a seat," he said, and gestured toward a pair of armchairs, which stood before a marble fireplace in one corner of the office. "I'd like to have a little chat."

"Well, that goes double for me." Janey eyed the pale blue watered silk, which covered the armchairs. She knew perfectly well that her jeans were as clean as they ever again could be, but here and there stains still marked the fabric. If any of them transferred to that delicate silk...

Then it was Webb Copeland's problem, she thought defiantly. She hadn't asked to be brought here. She sat down with a deliberately possessive thump, the kind that—when she'd been a teenager—had always made her mother cringe and plead for her to be more careful of the springs.

To her disappointment, Webb Copeland didn't flinch—he smiled. "Actually," he said gently, "I want to ask you a question." He sat down across from her, carefully adjusted the crease in his trousers, and leaned back in his chair. "Ms. Griffin, how would you like to be engaged to me for a while?"

CHAPTER TWO

WEBB COPELAND'S eyes were so wide and guileless, his smile so serene, and his voice so cool and deliberate that for a few seconds Janey didn't realize she was dealing with a man in the midst of a psychotic episode. And just how did one handle this particular variety of nutcase? Humor him? Try to reason things out? Scream and run?

"Engaged?" she managed to say. "You're certain that's what you meant to say? Because you surely don't mean engaged like the step before getting married—do you?"

"Not in this case. I mean, yes, that's exactly the kind of engagement I have in mind, but there's no question of marriage. That's the whole point."

Janey put the tips of two fingers against her temple and rubbed at a throbbing vein. "I think you'd better take it from the top, Mr. Copeland. And is there such a thing as a coffee machine at this end of the building? I think I'm going to need some."

He smiled. "Louise can no doubt find you a cup. Cream and sugar?"

"Just black."

He went to the door and called the secretary's name.

While his back was turned, Janey took a better look around the office. There was only one door, and Webb Copeland's body was still blocking it. But one wall was entirely glass, and though most of the windows were set solidly in place the bottom panels obviously opened for ventilation. They were shallow, but surely she could punch out the screen and slither through on her back...

23

On the other hand, Janey had never been the scream-and-run type. Honesty forced her to admit, however, that wasn't the reason she was sticking around. The truth was if she didn't hear all of this story she'd be lying awake every night for the rest of her life trying to figure it out.

Webb came back with two heavy ceramic mugs, which bore the Copeland Products logo. Janey was just a little disappointed to see that the cups were precisely the same as those in the employee break room. Wasn't that one of the perks of the executive wing—getting to drink out of real china?

The coffee was better, though—obviously fresh, which in her two months of working there had never been the case in the break room.

She held the mug in both hands. "You were saying?"

"Oh, yes, from the top." Webb sat down again. "Just over a year ago, my wife lost control of her car on an icy road and was killed."

"I'm sorry. I've heard about the accident, of course, but I'd forgotten." She saw his raised eyebrows and said, "Employees talk, Mr. Copeland."

"About my wife?"

Janey said dryly, "They talk about everything. If I'd known it was going to affect me personally, I'd have paid more attention to that particular story. At least, I assume you wouldn't be telling me unless it *is* going to affect me personally?"

He smiled a little, but he didn't answer directly. "Our daughter, Madeline, was less than two months old when her mother died."

"Oh." Janey hadn't heard that part of the story. "The poor child."

"She's doing quite well. She has a nurse, and my grand-mother moved in to provide a guiding hand." He sipped

his coffee. "That's the problem, actually—my grandmother. She's convinced I should get married again, for
Maddy's sake, and she's trying to persuade me."

Janey's eyebrows arched. "Come on, Mr. Copeland—
you have five hundred employees, and you don't have any
trouble at all bossing them around. Do you expect me to
believe you can't tell your grandmother to mind her own
business?"

"I have. And she's actually stopped talking about it—
the last time she brought up the subject directly was almost
three weeks ago. But ever since we had that last little chat
about how badly Madeline needs a stepmother, my house
hasn't been a safe place for me to go near."

Janey frowned. "Because you told her off? If she's so
angry—"

"Oh, she's far from angry. She's just determined, and
she's turned my house into a social center. That's fine with
me—she has a right to entertain her friends. It's just that
all of her friends suddenly seem to be single, under thirty,
and pretty in varying degrees. If I go home in time to play
with Maddy before her bedtime, I'm shanghaied into join-
ing Gran and one or another of her young lovelies at dinner."

"That's why you were working so late last night?"

He nodded. "I was dodging a blonde. Luckily I spotted
her before Gran saw me, so I escaped the dinner routine.
But I barely made it out the door, and I expect the blonde
stayed the whole evening waiting for me to show up
again."

Thank you for giving me an excuse, he'd said last night
outside the infirmary. Janey was beginning to see what he'd
meant.

"I can't set foot inside my own door without being ambushed—but if I stay away, I don't see my baby girl at all.''

"I don't suppose you've considered shipping your grandmother off to a rest home and telling all her pals to visit her there?"

He laughed, without much humor. "It's painfully apparent that you've never met my grandmother, Janey."

"All right, so I don't have an answer for you. You might try dragging her to a counselor, I suppose, but other than that—"

"Oh, there's a much simpler way. I'm going to give her precisely what she's asked for."

"Perhaps I've missed something," Janey mused. "But I think you just said you're going to get married to keep her from pushing you to get married, and somehow that just doesn't—"

"Not exactly. I'm going to introduce her to the woman I've chosen to be Maddy's stepmother—and, incidentally, my wife."

Janey crossed her legs and let her foot swing free. "I still don't see why I come into this."

"You're perfect," he said calmly. "She'll hate you."

Janey's foot stopped in midswing. She stared at the oversized, rounded toe of her reinforced shoes. "Because I'm so different from the ladies on her list?"

"Exactly. She'll be horrified, in fact."

She could almost see his grandmother now—eagle-eyed, upright, impatient to pounce on the slightest gaffe, ready to judge anyone who didn't precisely meet her specifications. He was no doubt right, Janey thought—the woman *would* hate her. Of course, that fact didn't make his assessment of Janey any more flattering... "And then, after a while, you'll break it off."

He nodded. "And Gran will be so relieved—"

Janey finished his sentence. "—that she'll start right in again. I don't know what you think you're going to gain in the long run."

"Oh, no, she won't. Because, you see, once she realizes the lengths I'll go to, she won't dare push me, ever again."

"You mean you're going to tell her the whole thing? Confess that it was a scam?"

"Of course not. She has to believe that I'd have gone through with it, or the whole operation's a waste." His eyebrows drew together. "It means, of course, that you'll have to be the one to break it all off—or at least it'll have to look as if you're the one."

"Leaving you with a broken heart," Janey mused. "Which in itself would buy you a little time, I suppose." She nibbled her thumbnail as she thought it over. She could see all kinds of flaws in this scheme—but then he hadn't asked her to critique his plan, only to pretend for a while to be his fiancée. She folded her arms across her chest, looked him straight in the eye and said bluntly, "So what's in it for me?"

He looked just a little shocked, and she wondered if it was her implied agreement or the brusque question that had startled him. Or was he just surprised that she needed to ask?

"If you say my job's hanging on whether I cooperate—" she began suspiciously.

"Of course not. That would be sexual harassment."

"Well, it's good to know *somebody* in this company knows the definition," Janey muttered. "So what are you offering?"

He countered, "What do you have in mind?"

She slowly finished her coffee while she thought it over, and then she set her cup down and said, "Money, of course."

Suddenly his eyes were as chilly as storm clouds.

What on earth did he expect? Janey thought, half-amused. He'd already classified her as ignorant, uneducated and socially inept—so why shouldn't she be a fortune hunter, too?

"And rather a lot of it." She told him exactly how much.

He swallowed hard. "Well, you're right about it being a lot."

Janey relented. Being paid for her work was one thing, but the figure she'd quoted was closer to blackmail—and she'd never intended for him to give it to her outright, anyway. She might not be able to borrow money from standard sources, but with her cooperation as collateral...why not? He could afford it. "We'll call it an interest-free loan, and—let me think—in about three years I can start paying it back."

"Of course you will." There was only a hint of sarcasm in his voice, but it rasped on her like tree bark against tender skin. "And why are we waiting three years? What's this *loan* intended for?"

Janey shrugged. "I don't see that it's any of your business how I spend it. If you're worried about me paying it off, you'll just have to rely on my character." She smiled sweetly and added, "Of course, if you're not happy with the arrangements, we don't have to continue this discussion at all."

He let the subject hang in the silent office until Janey concluded that she'd pushed him too far. *Oh, well,* she thought. *It was a great opportunity while it lasted.* She'd gambled and lost, and there was no sense in feeling disappointed. She wasn't any worse off than she'd been before she walked into his office.

He said, "It's a deal."

Janey could hardly believe she'd heard him right. Relief

and satisfaction—and a bit of fear at the job she'd taken on—surged through her.

His voice was brisk. "I want to get started right away. I'll break the news to Gran tonight, and you can come for dinner tomorrow to meet her. Seven-thirty—"

Janey shook her head. "Can't. Remember? I work the swing shift."

He lifted one dark eyebrow. "I assumed, with all that cash coming in, you'd be quitting your job."

She could, of course. With the assurance of that money—enough, she'd carefully calculated, to pay her tuition and support her adequately, though not luxuriously, through the rest of her education—she didn't need to work another day. She didn't need to face her fellow employees again, or crush her skull with those horrible electronic earmuffs, or ride the bus across town in the middle of the night...

On the other hand, there was as yet no guarantee that she'd actually be laying her hands on Webb Copeland's cash. That would depend on the success of this con, so she didn't dare let go of the security her paycheck offered quite yet—and with the hope that the end was near, she could put up with it for a while longer, anyway.

"I think I'll keep working for now," she said.

He took a deep breath, but he didn't argue the point. "All right. Lunch, then."

Janey consulted her internal calendar. Tomorrow was Wednesday, the day before the Thanksgiving holiday, so all afternoon classes had been canceled. "It'll have to be on the late side—like one o'clock."

"That'll work. I'll pick you up." He stood, obviously dismissing her.

Janey stayed firmly in her chair. "How does one dress to meet your grandmother?"

His gaze drifted slowly down the length of her body.

"How about your work clothes, and after lunch I'll drop you off here in time for your shift?"

"Don't you think that would be just a little obvious? I thought I'd settle for painting my face like a clown and stuffing all the tissue I can find down the front of a strapless sequined dress."

Webb smiled. It was, Janey thought, the first time she'd seen him display honest humor, and it looked good on him. The tiny lines around his eyes crinkled and his eyes glowed...

And that's enough of that, she told herself. He was the boss, he had hired her to do a job and she wasn't getting paid in smiles.

After she was gone, Webb called his secretary in. "You can send this back to personnel," he said, pushing Janey's file across the desk. "And call my grandmother, please, and tell her I want to talk to her alone tonight, so she'd better kick all the wannabe brides out of my house."

Louise's lips twitched. "I'll rephrase that, if I may?" she murmured, and left without waiting for an answer.

Webb pushed his chair back, put his feet up on the corner of his desk and stared out the window. The whole thing had gone very well, he thought. If he'd constructed her himself, he couldn't have come up with a more delightful combination for this job than Janey Griffin. Not only was she smart-mouthed, hard-edged, and entirely lacking in tact—qualities guaranteed to send Camilla Copeland straight up the nearest wall—but she was very nicely pack-aged as well. Janey was not beautiful, of course; in that department she couldn't begin to compete with the women Camilla had been throwing at him. But even in her work clothes Janey was attractive enough—tall, slender, straight-backed, with curves in the right places and huge hazel eyes

and well-shaped little ears and a firm if stubborn small chin
and pleasant, ordinary brown hair—that his grandmother
wouldn't have to ponder the question of how she'd initially
captured Webb's attention.

There were some women, he told himself, that Gran simply wouldn't believe he could fall for, no matter how convincing a story she heard. Janey Griffin wasn't one of them.
And yet, as soon as Camilla ran up against the smart mouth,
the hard edges and the complete lack of tact...

And Janey was going to keep her job, too—just as he'd
hoped she would. The idea of a prospective granddaughter-
in-law who worked the swing shift on a manufacturing
line—moving, carving and bending steel—was guaranteed
to make Camilla turn purple. He'd been right. Janey
couldn't be more perfect.

He took his feet off his desk and got his trench coat from
the closet. Louise would have made that call by now—so
he might as well go home, play with his baby daughter and
shock the hell out of his grandmother.

He was looking forward to it.

Not only the supervisor but every worker on the line knew
that Janey was late because she'd been summoned by the
boss. And since Janey could hardly tell them what that
conversation had been about, she could only pretend not to
hear the comments that rippled across the factory floor.

Eventually, when she didn't respond, the remarks settled
back into a more normal pattern—still suggestive and an-
noying, but at least not actively cruel. And she'd been right
in thinking that with an end in sight it would be easier to
ignore the tasteless talk. Instead of two more years of this
nonsense, she only had...weeks, perhaps?

She'd forgotten to ask how long he expected this masquerade to run, but she knew it wouldn't be two years; the

fairy tale Webb Copeland intended to spin for his grand-mother couldn't possibly hold up that long.

And when the farce was played out, she'd be sitting pretty. With cash on hand to pay her expenses, there'd be no need for her to work. She could enjoy the rest of her education, instead of enduring it. She could soak up every drop of knowledge instead of skimming the surface.

She'd have to pay all that money back, of course—and she'd do it, no matter what it took. It was obvious that Webb Copeland hadn't believed for an instant that she intended to, but Janey regarded this loan exactly the same as if she'd gone to a bank. Apart from the matter of interest.

By the time she started making payments, she thought dreamily, she'd be working at a job she liked, and she wouldn't be trying to balance school along with it. And she'd positively enjoy making sure he got every last cent back, if only to see the look on his face when he had to admit that she'd meant her promise all along.

Suddenly Janey realized that, though the machines still roared, the human noise on the factory floor had dropped to almost nothing. The effect was positively spooky, for it was nearly midnight—and people usually made more noise, not less, as the shift ended and they were free to go home.

She glanced around the floor, trying to spot the reason for the sudden quiet, and had to stifle a groan when she saw Webb coming straight toward her, hands in the pockets of his trench coat. She turned back to her machine and didn't even look at him when he stopped beside her.

"Not you again," she said. "Do you have *any* idea how much trouble it's causing me to have you hanging around?"

He shrugged. "I just came to drive you home. Oh, and to give you this." He pulled a tiny box from his pocket, snapped it open and held it out, balanced on his open palm.

Inside the velvet box, against a bed of black satin, a ring sparkled. Its brilliant center stone—nearly the size of Janey's thumbnail—caught the overhead light and shattered it into rainbows, which danced across the factory floor. Half the employees on the line craned their necks to get a better look. The other half, Janey expected, would be along in a minute or two.

"Please tell me this is a zircon and not a diamond," she muttered.

"Telling you that wouldn't make it one. And the jeweler who just sold it to me wouldn't be at all flattered."

"Where did you find a jeweler at almost midnight? On second thought, I don't want to know."

"At home, watching the sports channel—but when I told him what I wanted, he was quite happy to meet me at the store. Don't you like it? I'd have let you choose, but I thought Gran would ask questions if you weren't wearing a ring tomorrow."

Janey considered braining him with the nearest piece of steel. "Whether I like it is not the point. It's bad enough you bought a rock the size of a lighthouse beacon—"

"Gran would really think something's fishy if I didn't."

Of course he was thinking of his grandmother. But then it hadn't even crossed Janey's mind that he might consider *her* tastes. "But why you brought the thing here—"

"You don't really believe our engagement is going to remain secret, do you?"

Janey looked around the factory floor at a hundred interested faces. "Not anymore," she said dryly.

"Now that I've broken the news to my grandmother, it'll spread like wildfire."

Too late to back out now. The thought was automatic, and puzzling. Why would she even think of backing out?

"I wouldn't bet on her being eager to announce it. Was telling her as much fun as you expected it to be?"

He gave her a long, speculative look. "As a matter of fact, it was. Come on, let's get out of here, and I'll tell you about it."

She'd have loved to tell him to go sit in the car and wait for her, but the night worker who was taking over from her was already standing beside the machine with his mouth hanging open, taking in every nuance. So Janey put away her safety equipment and got her coat.

Webb had left his car in the no-parking zone right by the door. "She was absolutely speechless," he said as he opened the door for Janey. "I told her over dinner that I'd found the woman of my dreams—and once she recovered from choking on her soup she took it quite well."

"That's good. I'd hate for you to have a heart attack on your conscience." She frowned. "If you *have* a conscience?"

He didn't seem to have heard. "Gran wanted to go to Coq Au Vin tomorrow—she says it's the only restaurant in town that can produce a lunch fit to celebrate an engagement."

"Look, Mr. Copeland, I really don't want to go on stage at some fancy restaurant without so much as a dress rehearsal, so—"

"Don't you think you should get in the habit of calling me Webb? It's no problem, anyway—I told her you'd rather come to the house, so you could spend some time with Madeline. And since Gran's a bit concerned because you don't know Maddy very well—"

"*Very well?* I've never laid eyes on the child."

"I've brought her to the office to show her off a few times. You could have seen her then."

"I'll try to remember that. I do hope there's only going

to be one child present, because I'd hate to pick out the wrong one to go gaga over.''

"If there's any doubt, look for brown eyes the size of Lake Michigan and you won't go wrong. That takes care of Maddy and the lunch date. Is there anything else we need to talk about?''

"Yes. How long do you expect this to take?''

"Anxious to get your money? It's almost the end of November now…I'd say by Christmas.''

"That's charming,'' Janey said. "Your grandmother's going to love her Christmas present this year—*not* getting me in her stocking.''

"And I won't even have to wrap it,'' Webb agreed cheerfully. "Oh, now I remember the other thing. We haven't coordinated our stories.''

"And she's going to want details, isn't she?''

"Well, she's not actually nosy, so I think we can gloss over a lot of it. All I've told her so far is that you work at Copeland Products, and we met there.''

"How'd she take it? My job, I mean.''

"I didn't tell her exactly *where* you worked. I figured tomorrow was time enough for that.''

"How about if I just leave all the oil on my hands till then and you won't have to tell her anything at all?''

He looked at her almost sadly. "And you thought I was overdoing it with the work clothes? Anyway, I thought I should leave you as much leeway as possible. Stick to the truth as much as you can, though—I've found it's always safest. I'll just follow your lead.''

"And pick up the pieces?'' Janey said dryly. As Webb stopped the car in front of her apartment, she added, "Thanks for the ride home. It gives me just enough extra time to bleach my hair and paint my fingernails lime green.''

*   *   *

The apartment had no doorbell, so Webb rapped on the door and watched in fascination as several chunks of paint vibrated loose and floated to the ground.

When she opened the door, Janey was already wearing a coat, and Webb felt a tiny tinge of anxiety. She *had* been joking about wearing a strapless sequined dress, hadn't she? But she hadn't bleached her hair, though it seemed more gold today than the plain brown he'd thought it was. And even though it was once more pulled back in a French braid, it looked softer somehow than it had at the factory.

"I'd have been waiting outside," she said, "but I'm afraid this ring and this neighborhood are not a good combination." She waved her left hand; even in the shadowed basement stairway the diamond stood out like a searchlight.

"No lime green polish?" he asked, and was ashamed of himself for feeling relieved.

"Sorry to disappoint you, but my roommate used the last of the bottle just before I got home last night. She loaned me a dress to make up for it, though."

The tinge of anxiety grew stronger, but before he could say anything, Janey stepped outside and pulled the door shut.

"I'm surprised," she said as he slid behind the wheel, "that you didn't bring your grandmother along just so she could see the neighborhood. Or are you reserving that in case you need a knockout punch for later?"

She sounded a little testy, Webb thought. But of course she'd be nervous; even someone who knew what to expect would no doubt feel edgy about meeting Camilla Copeland for the first time. "Why do you live here, anyway? I know I'm not paying you a fortune—not yet, at any rate—but you make decent money."

She didn't look at him. "Because both Lakeshore

Towers and the Marina were full when I was looking for a place to live.''

Which meant she didn't want to tell him. Well, she obviously wasn't proud of the place—so maybe it just meant she'd gotten over her head in debt somehow and was ashamed of it. Of course, that didn't bode well for her promise to repay the phenomenal amount of money he'd agreed to give her when this was over. Not that he'd taken her seriously in the first place.

Considering the differences in the neighborhoods, it seemed an incredibly short distance from Janey's basement apartment to the Greek Revival mansion which the Copelands had handed down from generation to generation for more than a hundred years. Webb parked the car directly in front of the main door, in the elegant curve of the driveway, and turned to see Janey's reaction to his house.

All he could see was the back of her French braid. She was staring out the window, and he thought he heard her gulp.

He followed her gaze, wondering which feature had made the strongest impression on her. The half-dozen thirty-foot-tall Doric columns that framed the front portico? The classic egg-and-dart cornice just under the roof line? More likely it was the sheer size of the place that had awed her so.

He walked around the car to open her door. "It is a bit overwhelming, isn't it? I forget that myself sometimes, until I've been away from it awhile."

For a long moment he thought she hadn't heard him, and even when she pulled her gaze away from the house she seemed to have trouble focusing on his face. "This is incredible," she said. Her voice was shaky and little more than a breath.

He was beginning to feel a bit nervous himself, not so

much over facing his grandmother as for fear of what Janey might do. The last thing he'd expected was that the impertinent and brazen young woman he'd hired for this job would fall apart at the first challenge.

He took her arm and shook her just a little—gently, in case his grandmother might happen to be looking out a window. "Don't go to pieces on me now. You don't have to put on a show, after all. Just be yourself."

Janey stood her ground. "I wish I thought you meant that as a compliment." Her voice had once more taken on the acid edge he'd already come to expect from her.

Webb grinned. It'd be all right—she was back.

The butler opened the front door as they approached, and with a tiny bow he offered to take their coats. Janey didn't seem to notice; she stopped three steps inside the foyer, tipped her head back and stared up two full stories at the ceiling. "I hope you don't mind," she said. "But I'd never in my life have expected to see this."

Webb wasn't quite sure if she was talking to him or the butler, and he wasn't about to ask. He took hold of her coat collar and whispered, "Don't overdo it, all right?"

She let him slip her coat off, but Webb wasn't sure she'd heard him; she was gawking at the winding staircase when Camilla Copeland appeared in the door of the big parlor.

"Come *on*, darling," he said in a deliberate stage whisper.

Finally Janey blinked and seemed to return to earth.

Camilla had come forward with a hand outstretched. "I'm so pleased to meet you, Janey."

Webb thought her voice sounded a little strained, and he felt a momentary pang of conscience. But it was only momentary; after all, if it hadn't been for Camilla's less-than-subtle matchmaking efforts he'd never have dreamed of bringing Janey Griffin home to meet her. And it wasn't as if this state of affairs was going to last forever, anyway—just long enough for Camilla to get the message that if she tried to manipulate him, she wasn't going to like the results.

For the moment, he was simply pleased that they were off to a good beginning. Now if Janey carried through with her part...

"What a beautiful suit," Camilla said, and for the first time Webb dared to take a good look at what Janey was wearing.

It wasn't strapless, and it wasn't covered with sequins. In fact, her gray tweed skirt and jacket could have passed muster almost anywhere.

And yet it wasn't quite right, somehow. The skirt was shorter than fashion dictated, which probably meant that it was at least two years old. Camilla would notice that in a flash. And he was sure his grandmother hadn't missed the white camisole that peeked out from under the jacket, any more than he had. Lots of women were wearing them—but this one stood out from the crowd. Not only wasn't there much of it, but the silky fabric draped and the lace trim teased, and the combination made it quite obvious that it hadn't taken tissue paper to fill out Janey's figure. It was a wonder Camilla hadn't had apoplexy.

As far as the skirt was concerned, though, he had to admit that any woman with legs like Janey's would be foolish to keep them hidden—whether or not it was fashionable.

Janey smoothed a hand down over her skirt. "Thank you. I'll tell my roommate. I borrowed the whole outfit from her, because I didn't have anything nearly like it of my own."

Camilla's smile froze.

Webb wanted to applaud. Instead he decided to capitalize on the situation. "I'll bet you don't even own a dress, do you, Janey? I've never seen you wearing one. And you should have watched her practicing how to walk in heels, Gran. I haven't seen anything so funny in years. After wearing those heavy work shoes with the steel toes all the time—'' He paused, as if he was startled by Camilla's expression. ''Oh, did I forget to tell you, Gran, that Janey works in the factory at Copeland Products?''

Camilla looked as if she was trying to fight off a cramp. Webb turned to Janey to see if she was savoring the moment and was startled to catch a spark of irritation in her eyes.

''How very interesting.'' Camilla took a deep breath. ''Do come into the parlor, Janey. It'll be a few minutes until lunch is served, so let's take advantage of the chance to chat and get to know each other.'' She led the way.

Janey started to follow Camilla, but within three feet she'd stopped once more to look around. ''It's amazing, isn't it, that with the size of this space, voices don't echo.''

''It's an engineering feat,'' Webb said. ''Even though the walls look straight, they're actually curved just enough to push the sound on, not bounce it back. Believe me, you don't want the details. It's far too complicated.''

She looked straight at him, and though he didn't understand why, Webb felt icy tingles slither down his spine. He was glad Camilla was already in the parlor, settling herself in her favorite chair by the fireplace, too far away to get a good view of the face-off in the foyer.

Janey's voice was very low, and it was so sweet it could induce a diabetic coma all by itself. ''Too complicated for me to understand? Is that what you meant?''

''Not exactly. I just thought it was hardly your sort of—''

''And you probably also think I couldn't possibly comprehend that though this house is an extremely late example of the Greek revival style, it's architecturally significant not only because of the acoustical engineering techniques that Henry Bellows employed when he designed it but because it's one of the first residences he built with steel framing and not just timber and masonry. You're right—it's *completely* beyond me.''

She spun on her heel and swept into the parlor.

There wasn't an echo in the hall, he reminded himself. There never had been, for Henry Bellows's engineering skills had prevented it.

But Webb's ears were ringing nevertheless.

CHAPTER THREE

EVEN before she'd crossed the sea of oriental carpet to where Camilla Copeland was sitting by the fireplace, Janey had already admitted to herself that telling Webb off almost under his grandmother's nose probably hadn't been the smartest thing she'd ever done.

But it had certainly felt good.

She took the chair Camilla indicated and held out her hands to the crackling fire. "Wood fires are so beautiful," she said, "and so welcome on a gray day like this."

"Then you aren't a fan of gas logs? I've never liked them." Camilla smiled. "But then I'm not the one who has to carry the wood inside or the ashes out, so perhaps I have a biased view of the subject." She looked up. "Webb, why don't you get Janey a sherry? Or something else—I'm sure you know better than I what she'd like."

With her back turned to the room, Janey hadn't heard Webb approach, and when she caught sight of him, she thought he looked as if he could quite cheerfully drop cyanide in whatever beverage she chose. She shook her head. "Thanks, but I'm not much of a sherry drinker. Or anything else, really. Working around the machines has made me much more careful."

Camilla nodded toward Janey's left hand. "You're being cautious with that ring as well, I hope." She picked up a mass of rose-colored yarn from a basket beside her chair and placidly began to knit.

Janey looked down at the brilliant diamond. Last night under the factory lights it had looked almost garish. Today, as the stone reflected the flickering flames, it seemed quieter, classic—and mysterious. "Of course I wouldn't put something this valuable at risk."

Camilla shook her head. "No, that's not what I meant. Years ago my father-in-law nearly lost a finger when one of the machines caught his lodge ring. Smashed it almost flat. The ring, I mean—though the finger was pretty well crushed, too."

Webb poured a tiny glass of golden liquid for Camilla from the drinks tray, and set it on the table by her elbow. "Gran would be much more sympathetic if it had been his wedding band instead of a symbol of his mens' club." His voice was dry.

Was he going to pretend the whole exchange in the hallway had never happened? Eager to seize her cue, Janey looked up at him with a quick smile. But he obviously hadn't intended the remark to be humorous, for his eyes were still chilly. He leaned against the mantel with his arms folded across his chest. He was looking at her, Janey thought, as if she'd suddenly turned into a malaria-carrying mosquito and he was figuring out how to swat her. She began to wish she'd accepted a drink anyway, just so she'd have the glass to keep her hands busy.

Camilla daintily sipped her sherry and returned to her knitting. "I'm so glad you like the house, Janey. How thoroughly unpleasant it would be to live somewhere you didn't care for—and I'm afraid Webb would never give this place up."

For an instant, Janey's breath caught. But perhaps she was being too sensitive? Camilla's first sight of her had been as Janey stared around the hall; the woman would have to be dense as a tree trunk not to have realized at a glance that Janey had been thoroughly impressed. It didn't mean she'd overheard any of that squabble in the foyer.

Reassured, Janey found herself wondering how the dream girl Webb thought he'd hired would respond to that comment. *"It's just the right size to hold all my relatives— at least the ones who'll be living with us"*?

"It's awe-inspiring," she said finally. "Almost like a museum."

"I remember that feeling when I came here as a bride."

Was there the slightest trace of acid in Camilla's voice?

Camilla looked up from her knitting, her eyes bright and inquisitive. "It sounded just now as if you've made a special study of Henry Bellows, Janey. He's dear to our hearts, of course, but compared to the more famous architects who worked in the Chicago area he's almost an unknown."

Janey's throat closed up till she was absolutely sure she'd never be able to draw a breath again. She had underestimated the acoustics of the hallway; it might not echo, but it obviously made even a whisper carry—for it was apparent Camilla Copeland *had* overheard a good part of that low-voiced exchange.

The only comfort Janey could find was Webb's stunned look; he was obviously as startled as she was.

Terrific, she thought. Now he was furious *and* surprised. She'd really done it up big.

Camilla went on, calmly, "Architecture is one of Webb's favorite subjects, I know—I think the interest has been handed down in the genes ever since his great-grandfather commissioned this house. Was it the love of buildings which brought you together? And how, I wonder, did that subject happen to come up on the assembly line?"

Janey reflected, almost calmly, that hers was likely to be the shortest engagement in the history of western civilization. She waited for Webb to say something that would squash her as completely as his great-grandfather's ring.

But he was silent, apparently unwilling to step in—either

to rescue her or put her out of her misery. And it was far too late for Janey to play dumb on the subject, for she didn't dare take the chance of underestimating precisely how much Camilla had heard.

"My faculty adviser in the college of architecture is a Bellows fan," she admitted. "He's always using examples of his work—just a few months ago when we were studying acoustical engineering he got almost poetic about your foyer."

Webb looked as if he were strangling.

"Of course, when I first heard about this house, I never expected to see the interior."

"Webb must give you the complete tour after lunch," Camilla said.

Webb pushed himself away from the fireplace. "Oh, why don't we begin right now? Mrs. Wilson must be getting anxious to start her afternoon off, anyway, so let's go get Madeline—shall we, Janey?"

It was less a question than a growled order. Janey cast an apologetic smile at Camilla. "I've been so anxious to see her nursery," she offered. Webb's hand closed on her arm and she had to hurry her step to keep pace with him.

He'd learned his lesson about holding private conversations in the hallway, Janey deduced. Instead he practically dragged her up the stairs and into an alcove in the upper hall, where he released her, planted his hands on his hips and glared at her.

"I had no idea she could hear me," Janey said.

"Great excuse that is!"

"Well, you didn't, either," she said reasonably. "That was obvious."

"What the hell happened? You took one look at the house, fell in love with it and decided to go for broke? Or did you already have this planned before you even got here?''

"Go for broke?" Janey frowned. "You mean try to marry you for real, in order to get this house? Not a chance. Not even a Henry Bellows masterpiece would be worth putting up with you."

"You lied to me."

Janey faced him squarely. "I did not. You never asked about my background—you simply assumed because of my job that I'd climbed out of the primordial ooze just last week. *'Janey doesn't own a dress. You should have seen her trying to learn to walk in heels!'*" Her voice was bitter. "What were you planning to say next, I wonder? *'Of course I'll have to teach her to read and write'?*"

"That's not what I said."

"Maybe not the words, but it's exactly what you meant."

He looked a little ashamed of himself. "All right," he admitted. "It's what I wanted Gran to think, and maybe I went a little overboard. But what happened to playing your part?"

"I don't have to have hayseeds sprouting in my hair to get the message across that we're all wrong for each other. So what if I'm not quite the poster girl for ignorance and poverty? She's still going to hate me, Webb."

He looked as if he'd really like to believe her but didn't quite dare.

Janey caught a glimpse of movement in one of the long hallways that stretched away from the staircase seemingly into infinity. She turned her head just as a woman who was wearing a heavy coat and carrying a dark-haired child in a red velvet dress came into sight.

Webb looked over Janey's shoulder and said pleasantly, "Mrs. Wilson. I was just coming to get Maddy."

"And about time," the woman said flatly. "Or had you forgotten I'm supposed to have an afternoon out, not just a couple of hours?"

"I'm sorry. We were a little distracted downstairs."

Janey couldn't believe her ears. Webb Copeland was actually apologizing?

He took the child from the nurse's arms. Maddy snuggled close, and Mrs. Wilson pulled a pair of gloves from her pockets and briskly put them on. Her gaze slid over Janey, summarized and dismissed her. "Since I'm not leaving on time, I will of course be later getting back as well."

"Feel free to extend your time off as late as you like this evening," Webb said, and without answering the woman descended the stairs with her back rigid.

The child peeked at Janey from the safety of her father's arms. Her eyes were not only as enormous and dark as Webb had said they were, but at the moment they were overflowing with curiosity.

"Hi," Janey said gently, and Maddy hid her face again, her dark hair spilling over Webb's shoulder. "Does she talk?"

"She generally says each word once and stores it away," Webb said. "Except for *no*, of course." He shifted Maddy's weight so he could straighten her dress and the ruffled white tights underneath. "There's the lunch bell. We'd better get back downstairs before Gran sends out a search party."

Janey didn't move. "So what's the plan? Do I pretend not to recognize a napkin? Drink my coffee from the saucer?"

Webb shrugged. "Why are you consulting me all of a sudden? You're the one who's got all the good ideas. But get this, Griffin—don't you dare take a notion to strand me now. You made a commitment, and you're going through with this.''

''Why? Because it's too late to find a substitute rube?''

He didn't bother to answer, just started down the stairs. Behind his back, Janey stuck her tongue out at him. Maddy, looking over her father's shoulder, grinned at her.

Charmed, Janey made another face, and Maddy giggled.

Webb looked back and caught Janey midgrimace. She composed herself and caught up with him. ''I'll go through with it if you'll treat me like a human being,'' she offered.

She suspected he had to bite his tongue to keep from answering—and she thought it was just as well she couldn't hear what he was thinking.

After lunch, they moved back into the parlor for coffee, and Camilla asked when the wedding was to be.

''Not for quite a while,'' Webb said firmly.

''You can't wait long to set a firm date,'' Camilla insisted. ''There will be so much to do, and the good caterers and dance bands are booked ahead for months.''

Janey looked up from the plastic puzzle pieces that Madeline was piling in her lap. ''Webb doesn't want a big wedding.'' Surely it was safe to assume that, since what he really wanted was no wedding at all? ''And since I don't have much family anymore—''

''What Webb wants,'' his grandmother announced, ''is immaterial. The choice belongs to the bride.''

''Well, in that case perhaps we could...'' Janey took one look at the storm clouds in Webb's eyes and changed her mind; just now he wasn't likely to see humor in the idea of planning the world's most enormous wedding simply because all the complex arrangements could be used to postpone the eventual marriage—forever. She said hastily,

"We're really in no hurry. We want to give Maddy more of a chance to get used to me first."

Camilla glanced at the child, who was still retrieving puzzle pieces from the floor and awarding them one at a time to Janey. "Madeline doesn't seem to be worried about that," she said dryly. "And I'd think she could get used to you more easily if she saw more of you. Don't you agree, Webb?"

In the doorway, the butler cleared his throat. "Mr. Copeland, your secretary's on the phone. Something about an appointment."

Webb looked at his wristwatch and swore under his breath. "I'll take you home, Janey, so you can change for work."

"Heavens, no, my dear boy," Camilla said. "We've kept you away from your office quite long enough as it is without sending you on a side trip now."

Janey flipped a mental coin. Which would be worse—being left alone with Camilla, or being cooped up in a small space with Webb? She decided cowardice might be the best policy under these circumstances; he obviously hadn't yet had enough time to cool down after the shock Janey had given him, to say nothing of the fuel Camilla had been virtuously piling on the flames ever since.

"I don't want to hold you up, Webb," she said honestly. "I can take a bus—it's a pretty direct route and I'll have plenty of time."

"That settles it," Camilla said. "Run along, Webb." But he'd no sooner reached the door than she called, "Haven't you forgotten something, dear?"

Janey heard the almost-coy note in Camilla's voice and wanted to groan. Whatever was coming, she knew she wasn't going to like it; it was already obvious that the woman's acerbic moments were far preferable to her guile-less ones.

"I'm an old lady, Webb, and I have learned in my life-time that people who are going to be married sometimes kiss goodbye."

Webb said stiffly, "I didn't want to offend you, Gran."

"Well, I didn't suggest you throw Janey on the Oriental rug and ravish her right in front of me." Camilla's voice was tart. "I just meant that if you felt so inclined, you didn't need to hold off on my account. Or Madeline's, for that matter—the sooner she becomes accustomed to you showing affection to each other the easier it will be for all of you." She looked thoughtful. "Of course, if you *don't* feel like kissing Janey..."

"I always feel like kissing Janey," Webb said.

To Camilla, he probably just looked a little preoccupied, as if his mind was already on the business waiting for him. To Janey he looked like a man with a toothache. She knew the feeling quite well, herself.

It's no big deal, she thought. *A quick peck on the cheek—even from Webb—will be a whole lot less unpleasant than the average good-night kiss from a blind date.*

Webb leaned over her chair. His fingertips felt cool against her skin, sliding slowly from her temple down her cheek, turning her face toward him. His mouth barely brushed hers in a kiss that Janey thought probably looked convincing from across the room but was in fact more il-lusion than reality.

Janey started to say something light, like how much spice it added to have an observer, and realized too late that he hadn't intended that kiss as the main course but only the appetizer. Suddenly his lips were firm and warm against hers, and he seemed to intend to go on kissing her forever. The scent of his cologne made her head spin. Stunned, she stayed absolutely still while her entire consciousness narrowed down until the only thing she was aware of was the kiss.

His hand slipped to the back of her neck and pressed her even closer. *Kiss me back,* he seemed to be saying. *Make it look good.*

She moved not by her own will but in response to that insistent touch, tipping her head back, lifting her hand to caress his face, holding him close.

Now how do we get out of this? asked the last lucid fragment of Janey's brain, and as if in answer an indignant Maddy hauled herself up on the couch, plopped into Janey's lap, wriggled till she was squarely between them and held her arms up to her father.

Webb let go—or was it Janey who pulled away? She ignored the catch in her throat and tried to refocus her gaze on Camilla. "That's why we need to give Maddy some time," she said.

She thought Camilla might agree, with perhaps an ironic twist in her voice. Or she might frown…that wouldn't have startled Janey in the least.

But Camilla was smiling. Janey was shocked—until she realized that it wasn't a soft and romantic smile, a welcoming smile, or a reassuring smile.

Not at all. Instead Camilla looked triumphant.

Camilla wanted to call a cab to take her home, but Janey told her frankly that there wasn't room in her budget for taxi fare.

Camilla lifted one eyebrow. "I had no idea there still was such a thing as a young woman who doesn't hesitate to admit there's something she can't afford."

Janey wasn't quite sure how to take that. The words were almost complimentary, but the tone had been crisp. How did Camilla think she spent her money, anyway? Not that it mattered, Janey reminded herself, as long as she *didn't* approve. "I assume that means I now have your permission to take the bus?"

"Oh, no," Camilla assured her coolly. "It just means I'll have Albert pay the cabby when he picks you up," and before Janey recovered enough to protest, Camilla had already called in the butler and issued the orders.

Janey arrived at her apartment wanting nothing more than to lie down with a cold wet cloth on her forehead and forget the rest of the world—particularly the part that included Webb Copeland. But she wasn't allowed the luxury of even a few minutes alone; her roommate was sprawled on the living room couch watching a videotape of her favorite soap opera, and nearby her friend Ellen was sitting stiffly upright on a rickety chair.

"I hope you don't mind," Ellen said. "Kasey told me you had a business lunch and would be back before long, so I waited. I just need a couple of minutes..." Her voice trailed off. "Janey, please tell me you didn't go to a professional meeting in that suit."

"What's wrong with this suit? And be careful what you say—it belongs to Kasey, not me."

"That's some comfort," Ellen admitted. "At least it explains why the color's all wrong for you. You should never wear gray, you know. It's wonderful on Kasey, but not on you. With all the gold highlights in your hair, you ought to choose brown or cream or green—"

Kasey grinned. "She won't listen, you know. I told her the same thing."

"And that camisole," Ellen went on. "Your business people must have gotten an eyeful, with that neckline."

"Exactly." Not that it had seemed to matter, Janey reflected. Webb hadn't even seemed to notice her display of cleavage. Of course, she hadn't worn the camisole for his benefit but for his grandmother's...but he ought to have noticed anyway, if only to appreciate how subtly she'd displayed her bad taste. Instead he might as well have been looking at the crevices in Mount Rushmore. She unbuttoned her jacket.

"You mean you deliberately—" Ellen stopped dead.

Janey realized too late that Ellen was staring at her left hand, where Webb Copeland's diamond ring glittered fiercely in the light from the television screen.

Ellen took a long, deep breath. "And just what kind of business are you going into, girl?"

"Costume jewelry?" Janey offered hopefully. "It really looks like the genuine article, doesn't it? All I'll have to do is wear this stuff and people will buy it right off my hands. You don't believe a word I'm saying, do you?"

Ellen shook her head. "Looks to me like you've joined an escort service."

"Now that you mention it," Janey began.

"Except the guys who patronize those don't usually hand out diamond rings. So tell me, Janey—who's the guy?"

"Look, Ellen—if it's still going on in a day or two, I'll tell you, all right? Otherwise...well, believe me, this isn't a story you want to hear just half of, and I haven't got time for the whole thing right now, because I have to go to work."

Ellen said under her breath, "And I thought I had trouble with men."

I'll trade, Janey almost said, but something stopped her.

She didn't know what it was. It wasn't the thought of Webb, that was sure. Camilla, maybe? Under different circumstances, Janey could have liked the woman. Or Madeline—baby Maddy, who within minutes of her father's departure had snuggled in Janey's arms and gone to sleep?

She didn't know. The only thing she completely understood was how very confused she was.

Janey wasn't surprised, when she reported to her supervisor to start her shift, that he looked at her without enthusiasm and said, "The front office called down a message for you. The boss wants to see you in his office pronto."

Janey supposed she should have known better than to hope she could work a full eight hours without Webb interfering. The only question was why he was so anxious to talk to her. To announce his plans for following up the luncheon date? Or to call the whole thing off after all?

She hoped he wasn't canceling. She still needed the money. In fact, considering the downhill slide of her work performance, she was going to need it even worse.

She tugged her Copeland Products baseball cap down tighter on her head and turned toward the break room to return her safety equipment to her locker.

"Hey, Griffin," the supervisor called. "If you ever decide to actually work here again, let me know—okay?"

Janey growled to herself and took her time getting to the executive wing. Outside Webb's office, his secretary saw her coming and greeted her with a steaming coffee mug. She thanked Louise and opened the door without bothering to knock.

Webb's head was bent over the desk blotter, and the sight reminded her of how unexpectedly soft his hair had been. Her fingertips tingled at the memory.

Idiot, Janey told herself.

"Oh, sorry," she said when he looked up. "I got so much into playing my role that I forgot to be polite and announce myself."

"Knock it off, Janey." He folded a document, laid it aside and pointed toward the pair of armchairs by the fireplace. "We didn't have a chance to finish our conversation today."

So which was it going to be? she wondered. Would she walk out of this office with a new assignment for impressing Camilla—or without this extra job? She tried to joke away her sudden anxiety. "Really? I thought we'd pretty much exhausted the possibilities."

"On the contrary." He sounded a little grim. "We've hardly even begun."

She was an entirely different person than she'd been the last time she'd entered this office, Webb thought as he watched Janey move across the room.

Despite the heavy steel-toed shoes, she walked like a fashion model in elegant heels, with a slight but enticing sway of her hips. Despite the stained, worn jeans, she sat like a woman wearing an alluring short skirt. Despite the plaid flannel shirt, which concealed the cleavage she'd displayed so casually this afternoon, the glimpse of soft skin at the base of her throat—where the top button was open—intrigued. In fact, it was even more beguiling because it hinted instead of showing.

She wasn't like Sibyl, of course, and perhaps that had helped to mislead him. But then there were very few women as feminine as Sibyl had been.

Or was it he who had changed since yesterday? Had he looked at the same woman then and seen not the reality that was so obvious today but what he had wanted—what he *expected*—to see?

Not that it mattered precisely how he'd gotten into this mess. The bottom line was that he was stuck with her.

He poked at the fire till it flared up nicely, and sat down

across from her. "We need to decide how we're going to pursue this, Janey. Since you threw the original plan out the window today without even warning me—"

She interrupted. "*Are* we going to pursue this? I thought perhaps when you got away from Camilla and had a chance to reconsider—"

"I've reconsidered. And I've come to precisely the same conclusion I did earlier today—that I have no choice but to go through with it. Even if I announced right now that I was breaking off this engagement, my hands would be tied for months before I could try again to correct the situation."

"I can see," Janey mused, "that if you brought someone else home next week and told the same story, Camilla *might* be a little suspicious of your motives."

There was no missing the ripple of laughter in her voice. The least she could do, Webb thought grimly, was to take the whole thing seriously. Instead she seemed pleased to have him painted into a corner. Why hadn't he stopped to consider how much power he was putting into her hands?

"And in the meantime," he went on, "Gran would probably redouble her efforts to find someone who was both suitable and smart enough to trap me."

Janey smiled. "And, of course, silly enough to want you." She raised a hand to push a strand of hair back under the cap.

"Oh, thank you very much." His gaze sharpened. "Where's your ring?"

"Well, after that lecture this afternoon I'm not crazy enough to wear it to work—even if the rule forbidding jewelry wasn't made clear in the employee handbook."

"You didn't leave it in your apartment, did you?"

"So what are my options? Since everybody on the whole

shift has seen the damned thing, the first place anyone with sticky fingers would think to look would be my locker.''

She was right. And though he'd like to think that every one of his employees was completely honest, there was no guarantee.

"Don't sweat it, Webb. The rock's perfectly safe.''

"Where? Locked up in a pawnshop?''

Irritation flashed in her eyes. He was intrigued—suddenly they didn't look hazel at all but brilliant green. "What a shame I didn't think of that! I could hock it every night and reclaim it just in time for the next official performance. I'm ashamed of myself—the best I could think of was shoving it down in the bottom of a yogurt cup in my refrigerator.''

He thought for a second that he couldn't have heard her correctly. "You put a diamond ring in an empty yogurt cup in your—''

"Not at all. It's a full one. Apple granola, which my roommate hates—so there's no chance she'll mistake the ring for a particularly firm nut.''

Her eyes were sparkling like sunlight on seawater. She knew perfectly well she was yanking his chain, Webb thought, and she was enjoying it. Furthermore, there wasn't a single thing he could do to stop her—right now, at least.

Before this is over, he thought irritably, *I'll probably have strangled her.*

"And though I suppose it's discriminatory of me to make generalizations,'' Janey went on, "I doubt the local burglars are yogurt eaters, either, so—''

"All right, I'll take your word for it—but I'm holding you responsible for that ring.''

She smiled at him. "And what will you do if I lose it? Handcuff me to one of the factory machines till I pay it off? That'll only take a couple of decades.''

"No, I'll wait till you get your first big architectural commission and I'll seize your pay. Of course, if you don't carry out your part of this bargain to my satisfaction, I'll make sure you don't *have* any architectural commissions—big or small.''

Janey didn't look impressed. In fact, she delicately patted back a yawn.

Webb changed tactics. "So did Gran give you the full tour of the house after I left?''

The light in her eyes dimmed, and she sounded disappointed. "No. There wasn't time, if I was going to make it to work on schedule.'' Ostentatiously she looked at the mantel clock. "Of course, since I'm sitting here instead of working, it's apparent that it wouldn't have mattered if I was late. I should have taken her up on the offer to wander around and look my fill.''

"How long have you known about the house, anyway?''

"Last year. My professor just said it was a private residence, though—there was no owner's name attached, and he didn't even say which section of the city it was in. I had no idea it was yours till you stopped the car in front of it today.'' She leaned forward as if to challenge him. "Why? Are you still suspicious that I decided right then and there to turn myself into your grandmother's dream come true so she'd help me hook you for real?''

It did sound a bit silly, when he thought about it—that she'd even think such a trick was possible. And yet...

"You're being completely irrational, you know,'' Janey said. "If I wanted to—which I don't—I couldn't possibly make myself over into something that would suit her. I'm nowhere near your style, Webb.''

That was true enough, he thought. She wasn't his type. He just hoped Camilla saw it that way.

"But what you don't seem to realize is that your grandmother is not an idiot. I've just made your story a little less obvious, so she's more likely to believe it—that's all.'' She jumped up and stood by the fire, holding her hands out to the flame as if she was cold. "Anyway, what difference does it make whether she finds me unacceptable because I don't know the right fork to use, or because I won't hesitate to argue with her about Henry Bellows—he wasn't infallible, you know—or because I'm going to be a career woman and she wants Maddy to have a very traditional mom? The important thing is, I'm unacceptable—and she'll be enormously relieved when you finally tell her I'm history.''

The firelight flickered, casting shadows across her face. "You're quite certain of that.''

She wheeled around to face him. "Of course I'm sure. Good heavens, Webb, even Maddy's nurse spotted what a mismatch we'd be. Don't you think your grandmother has to have seen it?''

He didn't answer. Instead, very deliberately, he said, "Gran called me not long after you left the house.''

A tiny frown cut lines between her eyebrows. "You say that as if it's unusual.''

"She very seldom interrupts me at work, and when she does, there's always a point. This time she said, and I quote, 'No wonder you've been working late.' ''

"Oh.'' Her face brightened. "Maybe she was being sarcastic?''

"And she told me to invite you to stay with us for the long Thanksgiving weekend—since we're your family now.'' He paused to let the news sink in. "So let's try this again, Janey. What was it you were saying about how she's going to hate you?''

CHAPTER FOUR

JANEY stared at him for fifteen seconds, trying to fight off the giggles. But it proved impossible to hold her amusement inside, and ultimately she gave in to uncontrollable laughter, which lasted till she ached and had to hold her sides.

"I hope you don't make a habit of getting hysterical like this," Webb said coolly.

Janey sank into her chair and wiped tears from her eyes. "Oh, this isn't hysteria. This is sheer enjoyment."

"Well, I'm glad you find the invitation amusing, but—"

"*We're her family now.* I'll bet your grandmother sounded downright pious when she said that."

"As a matter of fact, she did. What's her tone of voice got to do with it?"

Janey wrinkled her nose in surprise. "Good Lord, Webb, don't you know *anything* about women? How long were you married?"

He said stiffly, "Just a little less than a year."

Janey sobered abruptly. Her question had been flippant, but the answer flooded her with sadness. He'd still been on his honeymoon when he'd lost his wife. No wonder Webb wasn't anxious to put anyone in—what *was* the woman's name?—her place.

Webb went on, "And that has no bearing on this situation."

"That's what you think." Janey's tone was gentler. "I knew it couldn't have been long, or you'd have picked up a few more clues about how the opposite sex thinks. Don't

60

you know what Camilla's doing? She's issued a challenge to me."

Webb looked at her as if she'd suddenly sprouted antlers. "Inviting you to stay with us for a weekend is a challenge?"

"Oh, yes. She's thrown down the glove—as much as announced that I'm going to have to earn my way into the family and I won't be getting any help from her to do it. But she's not about to let herself look like the bad guy—she has no intention of pointing out to you what a terrible choice you've made—because that would just make you more determined to follow through. So she's going to smooth the way for me—"

"I thought you said she *wasn't* going to help."

"Or, I should say, she'll at least make it look to you as if she's smoothing the way, so when I mess up you won't be able to escape seeing me as I truly am—inadequate, inappropriate, pathetic little me. Of course what she'll really be doing is taking every opportunity to sabotage me."

With a long whistle, Webb shook his head in something halfway between astonishment and admiration. "You actually got all that out of a two-sentence invitation to spend the weekend?"

"That and the fact that she used you as the messenger. She could have phoned me, but this way she makes herself look to you like the saint welcoming the stranger into the family fold. And, of course, I was expecting it, since she'd already started the campaign this afternoon."

"What? It didn't look to me as if she was discouraging. She practically flung her arms around you."

"No, she didn't. Weren't you listening to her tone of voice? And if you're judging by things like her promoting that silly goodbye kiss—well, if you thought that was approval, you didn't see the look of malicious triumph on her face. That was careless of us, by the way—we should have seen it coming.'' Janey shook her head in reluctant admiration. "Your grandmother is one stylish lady, Webb. She doesn't miss a trick.''

"The situation still doesn't strike me as funny.''

"Oh, it wouldn't be, if we were serious about each other. In fact, it would be downright unpleasant, with her creating all sorts of opportunities for me to make a fool of myself. While I was tripping over my feet trying to get every detail just right, she'd already have moved on and be busily setting up the next embarrassment.''

Webb said slowly, "But considering that we want you to look unsuitable...''

"Now you're getting it. Of course, she doesn't know that, which is where the humor comes in. I'll have loads of fun doing just as I please, and she'll be thrilled at the spectacle I'm making of myself and counting the minutes till she's rid of me.''

Of course, immediately after the breakup Camilla would start straight in with her parade of eligibles once more, hoping to catch Webb on the rebound before he fancied himself in love with another unsuitable woman. *But that's not my problem, is it?* Janey told herself.

"What kind of spectacle?'' Webb asked.

"You mean, what sort of embarrassments will she pull?'' Janey stared thoughtfully at the ceiling. "Oh, I'm betting she'll serve some really exotic foods and hope that I don't know how to eat them. Which, by the way, I probably won't. I've never met an artichoke, and I don't care if I never do. And of course there's the obvious—she'll introduce me to one of your old girlfriends, just to illustrate the contrast between her and me. And afterward she'll apologize to me, in front of you, for being rude in talking to her about people I've never heard of and places I've never been—just so neither of us will be in any doubt of how out of place I am in your world. Things like that."

"You really think Gran would—" He shook his head.

"You sound like a six-year-old who just learned the truth about Santa Claus," Janey said in exasperation. "Remember? This is the same woman who's been parading her list of beauties in front of you, arranging all those impromptu dinner dates."

"But setting out to make you look like a fool—"

"Oh, she's got a lot more class than to do it openly. She could swat me like a bug, but that would be too obvious. She's aiming to make you think it's your idea to dump me and save the family honor and money from a merciless fortune hunter."

"Which, come to think of it, you are."

The words stung, but Janey covered her irritation by thrusting out her chin. "I certainly am—college is a mighty expensive hobby. Not that I'm feeling defensive about my part of the bargain, because it's still a good deal for you— it comes out a lot cheaper in the long run than keeping a wife." She stood up. "Speaking of money, I'm so hungry for it that I'd better get to work before the supervisor hires someone else to fill my job. Just when does this weekend officially start?"

"I don't suppose you could find an excuse."

"She'd only come up with something worse."

"I suppose you're right. Dinner's at one so the staff can have the rest of the day off. I'll pick you up at noon."

"Fine. Bring your grandmother for a before-dinner drink, if you like. We don't have any sherry, but Kasey always keeps generic beer in the refrigerator—I'm sure she'd like that."

"I just want to get her off my back, Janey, not give her a stroke."

"In that case, we should probably save that invitation for the grand finale. And, Webb? Don't worry about the details—you can leave that to me. All you have to do is look a little bewildered from time to time." She smiled. "Sort of like you're doing right now. I expect you'll turn out to be a natural at it."

Camilla had gone out to a party, so to Maddy's delight, Webb unearthed his old tub toys and spent the better part of the evening launching one plastic boat after another, firing them across the nursery bathtub to her so she could pour each one full of water and sink it for him to retrieve and launch again. She insisted on staying in the tub till the water grew chilly and her teeth started to chatter, and then he wrapped her in a big terry towel and held her close till she was dry and warm again.

Was there anything, he wondered, that smelled sweeter than a newly bathed baby?

Because he was still a bit awkward with the hair dryer, he ended up with Maddy's fine hair standing on end atop her head. When Camilla came home from her party and popped in to kiss the baby good-night, she looked askance at the rooster tail of dark hair, but she didn't comment.

Webb zipped Maddy into her pink blanket sleeper and handed her over to Camilla for a hug. She held her close and said, "I thought Mrs. Wilson was supposed to be back by now."

"I told her she could be as late as she wanted tonight."

"Why? You put up with far too much from that woman. Of course, once you and Janey are married..." Camilla's voice trailed off into an inviting pause.

What was it Janey had said this afternoon, about his grandmother being annoyed at the idea of her being a career woman instead of a traditional mother figure? He might as well concede Camilla the point right now; the faster they moved along, the sooner this farce would be finished. "And I'll probably be putting up with her for a good while longer. Janey can hardly take a baby to class with her."

"Hmm," Camilla said, and that was all.

But he thought he saw a gleam of satisfaction in her eyes.

He supposed he shouldn't be surprised at the evidence that Janey was right—but he had to admit he was. Yes, Camilla had been scheming for the last month, but that had been open and obvious. This was a different sort of maneuvering altogether, the kind of plot that could get out of hand and hurt people. He hoped Janey knew what she was doing.

Though why should he worry about it? He was paying her—and paying her well—to do this job. Whether her ego was damaged in the process was her lookout, not his.

He sat down in the rocking chair and Maddy snuggled her face into his shoulder and fingered the satin edging of her blanket. "What do you think of her?" Webb asked.

"Janey?" Camilla appeared to think about it. "She's quite...interesting. Not much like Sibyl, of course." She patted Maddy's head, kissed Webb's cheek and left the nursery.

In the silence, broken only by the rhythmic squeak of the antique rocker, Webb sat with his daughter held close, watching her face as her eyelids grew heavier. She would be a beautiful woman, like her mother. He could see it already in her hair, her eyes, her heart-shaped face—all like Sibyl's.

When he closed his eyes, he could still see Sibyl's face, as clearly as the day she had died. *Not much like Sibyl,* Camilla had said of Janey. That was the understatement of the year.

He sat there rocking Maddy till long after she'd gone to

sleep, and when the nursery door opened he started a little himself.

Mrs. Wilson raised one plucked eyebrow. "And just how long has she been asleep?"

"I've already told you I don't think it hurts her to stay up a little later once in a while."

"Not as much as it does to sit and hold her while she sleeps," Mrs. Wilson snapped.

He felt just a trifle guilty—he'd meant to put Maddy in her crib, where she could sleep more soundly. He hadn't intended to sit there so long holding her, but his daughter's weight in his arms had been incredibly comforting. He laid the baby in her crib. She gave one tiny cry, and then lapsed into sleep again.

"She'll wake at least twice tonight wanting you," the nurse said. "She always does, when you've put her to bed."

Webb frowned. "You've never told me that."

"No, I've simply dealt with it."

His voice held an edge. "Well, next time you can deal with it by calling me." He leaned over the crib to pat Maddy's hair back into place, and tiptoed away.

Only the dim security lights still glowed downstairs; the winding staircase was shadowed. The door of Camilla's room was closed, which meant she had gone to bed.

In his room, the bed was already turned down and a pair of blue-and-white striped silk pajamas were neatly laid out next to the pillow. Webb grinned and moved them, just as neatly, to the top of the bureau. Tomorrow morning, the butler would put them in a drawer, and in the evening he'd lay them out again.

Albert denied having a sense of humor, but Webb didn't believe him—unless he saw the joke in the whole thing, he'd have given up on the pajamas long ago.

Silk pajamas belonged to the master bedroom, not the smaller room next door that Webb had claimed for himself. It had been a year since Sibyl died—but he had felt no desire to move back into the master suite. It had been very much Sibyl's room, and it was still full of her things, her scent…and the memories.

Sibyl.

Her car had slid out of control on the first ice to coat the streets last winter, the storm that always caused the most accidents because each year drivers had to teach themselves all over again how to maneuver on slick roads. Most of the accidents were only fender-benders; Sibyl's had been anything but. There hadn't been a recognizable fender left— and not much else, either—after her BMW had smacked into the concrete support that held a highway sign and then spun off the road and rolled down an embankment. They'd called him at midnight, but he hadn't made it to the hospital in time…

It was just half an hour till midnight now, and he found himself restless, staring out the windows, which overlooked the broad sweep of driveway. The night was crisp and clear, and the streets were clean and dry. At this hour, though, he always thought he could see the gleam of ice. Of danger.

Janey's shift would end soon, and she'd leave the factory and get on a crosstown bus. At least, he told himself, she wasn't wearing that ring; at this hour of the night, people had been murdered for a whole lot less.

He found himself grinning at the very thought of thousands of dollars worth of diamond resting at the bottom of a yogurt cup. Camilla was right, he thought. She *wasn't* much like Sibyl.

He got his coat and went down the stairs, through the kitchen to the garage. If he hurried, he'd get there just about the time she came out the door.

* * *

The last thing she'd expected to see was Webb's car, waiting just outside the employees' entrance. For an instant Janey wondered if she'd conjured up the sight, if she'd been thinking so gloomily about having to endure the fifteen-minute wait in the cold wind for the bus that she was seeing things that weren't really there.

She stumbled, and a man behind her bumped into her and growled something under his breath about how nobody was clearing the frost off his windshield, much less giving him a ride home in a preheated car.

Janey slid into the seat and turned to Webb. "I thought you said noon, not midnight."

"I did. I thought you might like a ride home."

"You're going to create yourself a lot of trouble."

"Well, if you don't *want* a ride—"

"It's not that. But somebody's going to start hollering discrimination pretty soon."

"It's discriminating against everyone else if I give my fiancée a ride home?"

"Well, maybe not that, exactly. But they're going to start wondering other things—like what extra kinds of special treatment I'm getting. My supervisor is already pretty put out—and as for the guys on the line…"

"It wouldn't hurt my feelings if you quit, you know."

Mine, either, she thought. The remarks she was overhearing weren't quite as crude as they'd been last week, and they weren't quite as open. But she hadn't anticipated the undercurrent of anger—it was a new development.

If she quit, however, and then for some reason his plan fell through…she'd be stranded with nothing.

"And save you the drive?" she said crisply. "Surely you aren't planning to make a habit of this?"

"I don't know. Will I have to?"

"Nobody asked you to."

He didn't respond to the aggressive note in her voice. "What time do you get home when you ride the bus?"

"Usually about a quarter to one. Why?"

"And then you catch a little sleep, go to classes all day, and go back to work at four in the afternoon. When do you study and write papers?"

"I fit it in between classes."

"I'll bet. You're right, college is an expensive hobby—in more ways than one. I shouldn't have made that crack about you being a fortune hunter."

Janey considered. "Does that mean you really believe I'm not trying to marry you after all?"

"You'd better not be. And don't get confused about what I'm feeling. It's nothing more than a little guilt that on top of everything else you're juggling, you've taken on my little job."

She was worn-out from the stress and sheer length of the day, or she probably wouldn't have reached across the car and playfully ruffled his hair and said, with a laugh in her voice, "Whatever you say, Webb. And if I change my mind about marrying you, you'll be the first to know."

The clock was ticking inexorably toward noon, while Janey fussed with her hair. She finally settled for bending over till her hair touched the floor and brushing it vigorously against the grain. The resulting shiny, bouncy mass was as far from Camilla's neat curls as Janey could manage.

Kasey wandered in with a doughnut in one hand and a cup of coffee in the other. "Do you want my mother's bourbon-flavored stuffing recipe to take with you? That would shock the old lady."

"Too late. The turkey must already be in the oven."

Kasey shrugged. "That's the best part of the idea, since the stuffing sounds better than it tastes."

"Which isn't saying much." Janey stood up straight and touched up the edges of the wild mane her hair had become. "I thought you were going to your parents' house for dinner today."

"I am. I'm just putting it off as long as possible, because it usually isn't just the turkey that gets stuffed with bourbon at our family parties."

Janey shot a concerned look at her, but Kasey seemed quite matter-of-fact. "I wish I could take you with me instead."

"No, you don't," Kasey said cheerfully. "You're only pretending to be a hick, while I really am one. The comparison would make you look great, which I gather is the last thing you want—right?"

Janey grinned. "You're pretty much wrong on all counts, but I don't have time just now to argue about it." Kasey had her rough edges, that was true—but as far as Janey was concerned, her sense of humor and her on-the-dot perception more than made up for the things she lacked.

"I'll settle for a blow-by-blow description when you get back. Sunday, you said?"

"I assume so. The invitation wasn't very specific—just 'the weekend.' Darn it, there's the door and I'm not ready. Will you go let His Highness in? Or better yet, leave him standing on the step."

Kasey grinned. "I'll show him my collection of paint-by-number masterpieces. Or shall I tell him they're yours? That ought to leave him speechless."

Janey could hear the murmur of voices through the thin walls, but she couldn't distinguish what was being said. She finished applying her eye shadow, picked up her overnight case and her backpack full of books, and strolled out to meet Webb.

He was standing in the middle of the living room with Maddy, bundled up in a yellow snowsuit, in his arms.

Janey was startled. He'd said he was doing this so he wouldn't have to dodge Camilla's lovelies in order to have time with his daughter, but nothing Janey had seen yesterday had implied he was much of a hands-on father. He'd left Maddy in the nursery till the last possible moment. At lunch, it was Camilla who'd supervised as Maddy played with a few carrots and a cup of spinach dip, Camilla who explained that the child had already had lunch upstairs. And though later Maddy had toddled from one adult to the next in her play, it was the newcomer who had seemed to fascinate her. She hadn't even shown any possessiveness till her father had kissed Janey. In fact, she'd treated him more like a climbing gym—big, handy, secure and constantly challenging.

Which made perfect sense, now that Janey stopped to think about it. A child who didn't see her father much wouldn't behave that way; she'd be more likely to be wary.

And hadn't he told Janey that he'd brought Maddy to the office several times? But she'd been too preoccupied just then with the reality of facing Camilla to pay much attention, so her image of Webb as a distant parent had gone undisturbed.

Of course now she was basing her opinion on scant evidence, too. The fact that he'd brought his daughter on a car ride didn't exactly mean he spent countless hours with her.

He turned around as she came in. He was dressed more casually than she'd ever seen him before, in an open-neck shirt and heavy sweater, dark trousers and a black leather jacket, which looked buttery soft.

"Sorry to be late," Janey said. "I don't even have the excuse of not being able to decide what to wear, because this is basically it." She flicked a hand down her jade green twill trousers, which she'd teamed with a beige-and-green sweater from Kasey's collection. "After all that fuss I made yesterday about you saying I didn't own a dress…well, this morning I had to admit it. I don't. So after today, it's going to be jeans."

Babbling, she thought. *That's a good one to remember. Me running off at the mouth like this would probably drive Camilla straight to the sherry bottle.*

It obviously wasn't doing much for Webb, either. He looked tired this morning, she thought. She wondered if, despite the holiday, he'd been in the office for a while. She wasn't the only one who was missing hours and hours of work all of a sudden, she reminded herself. By arranging their lunch yesterday to fit her schedule, he'd taken the heart out of his own day.

She flicked a gentle finger against the baby's cheek. "Hi, Maddy. You look like a snow bunny today—all you need is skis."

"Want me to take that backpack?" Webb asked.

"And carry the baby, too?" Janey shook her head. "I'm used to it. I do hope Camilla hates jeans, because she's going to get her fill of them this weekend."

"She's never said anything about mine—but then I don't have time to wear them much. And I don't think Sibyl owned a pair."

Sibyl. Of course the woman would have a name like that, Janey thought. All glamour and elegance and mystery. Janey could almost picture her, too—not her features so much as the general look. Without a doubt she'd been sleek and graceful and cultivated—all the things Janey could never be.

Which, of course, was precisely why she—Janey—was

going off to spend the weekend with Webb Copeland's family. Because she was so incredibly different.

And that, she told herself, was simply a fact of life—and the tighter she held on to the knowledge the safer she'd be.

"Anything else?" Webb asked.

"I don't think…oh, the ring. I knew I should have gotten it out last night—I almost forgot." She headed for the kitchenette, which occupied a corner of the living room, screened only by a low bookcase, which served as a divider, and opened the refrigerator. With a chopstick she fished in the bottom of the yogurt cup and retrieved the ring, which came out not only coated with off-white goop but with a deformed raisin hanging from one of the prongs that held the diamond.

Webb looked as if he was in pain.

"Sorry," Janey said. "I really didn't intend for you to see this." She held the ring under the tap till the water ran clear, the gold gleamed, and the diamond was once more brilliant. She dried it off and slipped it on her finger. "Not bad," she said. "In fact, it's amazingly shiny. Maybe that's the next incredible household tip."

"Using yogurt to clean jewelry? I doubt it'll catch on."

In the car, she fiddled with the ring and finally asked, "Webb, is there anything I should know before the weekend?"

"Like what?"

"I don't know what," she said unhappily. "Things your grandmother would expect you to have told me. Things I'd have insisted on knowing. Like…oh, like when Maddy's birthday is."

"The end of September."

"And yours?"

"March. So you don't have to worry about surprise parties for either of us."

"Too bad. It would have made the perfect opportunity to shock your grandmother."

"By having a stripper burst out of a cake?"

"Oh, no. I'd have thought of something a lot more original—and worse—than that. Did she and Sibyl get along?"

"Of course."

The certainty in his voice, in the lift of his eyebrows—as if he was surprised she'd bothered to ask—grated on Janey's nerves. "But then your grandmother wasn't living with you, was she? Didn't you say she moved in after the accident, to oversee things for Maddy?"

In the back seat, strapped safely in, Maddy gave a happy little crow at the sound of her name.

Janey twisted round to smile at her. "So they weren't sharing a breakfast table every morning? That kind of thing makes a difference sometimes. Of course, you can love people immensely and still not be able to live with them."

"They liked each other just fine. Sibyl's parents were friends of Gran's." Webb's tone was repressive.

What a surprise, Janey wanted to say. No doubt that explained why Camilla had chosen the young women she had to parade in front of Webb—she was trying to find someone just like Sibyl to take her place. And perhaps, she speculated, Camilla was only doing what she'd done before. If she'd been instrumental in arranging Webb's first marriage, to the daughter of her friends—well, why should she hesitate to try it again?

The blocks had sped by, and before she could press for more the car drew up in front of the house. Webb unbuckled Maddy and lifted her out; Janey took advantage of the delay to once more feast her eyes on Henry Bellows's design. Yesterday she'd been too much in shock to really study the lines, and the pictures her professor had shown in class didn't begin to do justice to the house. The place was mammoth, she knew—and yet, imposing as it was, the perfect proportions of the exterior kept it from overwhelming the entire neighborhood.

Webb was unbundling Maddy from her snowsuit when Camilla came down the stairs. "Hello, Janey. I'm glad you could join us for the holiday."

"Thank you for inviting me, Mrs. Copeland."

"Nonsense, dear, call me Camilla. It'll be much less complicated when you're Mrs. Copeland yourself." She looked down at the baby. "Which reminds me—what about Maddy?"

A chill crept with torturous slowness up Janey's spine.

"I forgot to ask what you'd like her to call you. It'll be far easier if you start correctly from the beginning, you know, instead of trying to change it later. So will it be Mama, or Mommy?"

The chill hit the back of Janey's neck and gave her an instant headache. So Camilla wasn't going to bother with little things like artichokes and old girlfriends, was she? She was going straight for the jugular, forcing Webb to think about his child calling Janey Mother, in place of the beloved Sibyl...

Maddy's forehead wrinkled. "Ma," she said, smiled triumphantly and waved both hands in excitement.

Camilla glanced past Janey to Webb, and Janey saw satisfaction glimmer in her eyes for one instant before she smothered it.

And no wonder she seemed gratified, Janey thought—for Webb looked dazed, like a man who'd just shaken a feather pillow without knowing there was a hole in it, and who was now faced with the problem of gathering all the bits of down that had escaped and stuffing them back in.

CHAPTER FIVE

JANEY scrambled for an answer. She cringed at the thought of encouraging a child to call her Mother—in whatever form—when she had no intention of filling that position. But surely the mere word couldn't have much meaning to Maddy, who hadn't had a mother since she was a couple of months old?

And this craziness surely wasn't going to go on long enough to give Maddy a complex, was it? In a matter of weeks—maybe just days—Janey would be only a vague memory. And she already knew better than to get attached to this little girl, or to allow Maddy to get attached to her. She'd walk away, and Maddy would soon forget about the woman she'd briefly called Mama and...

No. The word was simply too special to be taken in vain—no matter what. Janey tried to sound casual. "Oh, for just now, let's stick to my name, I think."

Camilla's elegantly arched eyebrows rose ever so slightly.

Janey told herself that the less said the better; explaining was always dangerous. But her tongue seemed to have a mind of its own. "Even as young as Maddy is, I'd feel uncomfortable trying to take over Sibyl's place altogether. For one thing, I couldn't do it—"

The expression on Webb's face seemed to confirm that, Janey thought. She hoped that Camilla would think he was merely annoyed with the multitude of fastenings on Maddy's snowsuit.

She plunged on, not sure whether she was making things

76

better or worse. "And I'd hate to have Maddy think some-day that I'd tried to wipe her mother out of her life alto-gether."

Finally Webb managed to get Maddy free. "Who designs these things, anyway? People who have never tried to dress babies, that's sure." He set Maddy on her feet in the middle of the patterned marble floor. "Perhaps we should let the whole subject rest till Maddy can decide for herself."

Janey felt as if he'd thrown her a life belt. "Absolutely." She flashed a smile at him. "*Mama* is a title to be earned, anyway—not one to be handed out lightly." She bent over Maddy. "So you think about it hard, all right, Madeline?"

"Ma," Maddy said, and grinned.

"It appears," Camilla murmured, "that she's already de-cided. Janey, let me show you up to your room. Albert will see that your luggage is brought up later." Without waiting for a reply, or even glancing at the battered old overnight bag or the almost-threadbare backpack, which still sat just inside the door, she turned toward the winding staircase.

Janey thought that calling those bags "luggage" was the epitome of tact. If they'd been made of newly polished alligator, Camilla couldn't have been any more respectful.

As they reached the top of the stairs, Camilla waved a hand casually toward the hall to their left. "Webb's room is there, of course."

And what does she think I'll do with that information, Janey wondered. *Sneak in to visit him?* And, if so, was Camilla warning her or giving tacit approval?

You, Janey told herself, *have been exposed to far too many of Kasey's soap operas. You're beginning to sound like one.*

She managed a fairly good look down the length of the hall, since the main door that closed off the entire wing stood open at the moment. From the look of it, the master suite was about three times the size of her entire apartment, and a whole lot nicer—she could see the faint gleam of light against a subtle tapestry wallpaper in the hallway, and the corner of what looked like a very good painting.

"That's one of many things we'll need to do this weekend," Camilla went on. "Of course you'll want to redecorate the master bedroom—perhaps the entire suite. And these things take so much time."

Janey suspected Camilla hoped it would take forever—or at least long enough for Webb to get over his supposed enchantment. Nevertheless, she seized on the excuse. "Oh, yes—it would be much better to have a completely new look. Much more comfortable for Webb." She managed what she hoped sounded like shy modesty. "And for me, of course. If Sibyl was anything like the glamorous woman she sounds like…"

Camilla paused and looked Janey over from head to foot. "She was." She turned down the hallway leading to the opposite end of the house from the master suite.

It was perfectly clear to Janey what she was thinking. *And you're not.* Not that Camilla would ever come straight out and say it, of course. Her silence wouldn't be because she was diplomatic, though, but because the fact was so clear there was no need.

If this battle was for real, Janey thought, *I'd be crawling off to the field hospital by now.* If she had really cared for Webb and seriously wanted to take Sibyl's place, that remark wouldn't have just stung, it would have devastated. As it was, she could shrug it off and fire a shot of her own.

"It'll take forever, I suppose. All those decisions to be made, and all the work to be done." Janey sighed. "I know it's only sensible to put off the wedding for a while, but sometimes the idea of waiting…" She let the thought dangle, certain that Camilla would have no trouble filling in the blanks. *I'm anxious to get my man so he can't change his mind*—any of a hundred variations on that theme would do just fine.

"Of course," Camilla said thoughtfully, "the house *does* have eight bedrooms, so if Webb was truly in a hurry..." She pushed open a door. "This is the yellow room. I thought you'd like it best because of the garden view."

Janey hardly heard her. The woman is a master, she thought. To have taken what Janey had implied and so quickly turned it around—as much as saying that Webb must already be having grave doubts or he'd at least be setting a wedding date—was an incredible performance.

By the time Janey managed to pull herself together, Camilla had strolled across the room and opened the sheer curtains. "Even with the leaves and flowers gone and the winter mulch in place," she mused, "I still think the garden's attractive in a minimalist sort of way."

"Lovely," Janey managed to say. "It's like the difference between an ink drawing and an oil painting—they're both beautiful, but utterly different." In the faint reflection in the window, she thought she saw Camilla smother a tiny smile, but by the time she turned there was nothing to see.

The room was not enormous, but it was pleasantly spacious, with a four-poster bed and a pair of comfortable-looking chairs placed to have a garden view. The carpet and chairs were forest green, the draperies and comforter pale yellow. On a sunny day, Janey thought, it must look like a forest bower. Even in November's gloom, it would be difficult not to find one's spirits lifted here.

"The bath is through there." Camilla pointed. "When I checked this morning it seemed everything was in place, but if there is anything you don't have, I'm just across the hall."

I wouldn't dare need anything, Janey thought.

"There's the lunch bell," Camilla said. "Albert's a bit early today, I think—he must be anxious to be off to his sister's house for their family celebration. Shall we go down?" At the door she waved a hand toward the end of the house, beyond Janey's room and on down the hall. "Madeline's nursery is at the end and just around the corner."

Just around the corner? It looked to Janey as if it was located in outer Mongolia—certainly as far as possible from Webb's bedroom. "I thought the nursery would be part of the master suite."

Camilla's eyebrows threatened to join her hairline. "My dear…with a nurse in attendance?"

Janey felt herself flush. It had been a perfectly silly thing to say, of course, and yet… "Just call me inexperienced," she said sweetly. "Where I came from, people took care of their own kids. And they didn't like walking half a mile in the middle of the night to do it, either."

"And where was that?" Camilla asked politely as they walked down the hall toward the staircase.

"Where I came from? Downstate Illinois—a little town you've probably never heard of. Elmwood's so small, in fact, that this wouldn't be called a house, or even a mansion. It would be known as a neighborhood."

Camilla actually smiled at that. Janey felt rewarded.

"And what did your parents do? Are they no longer living?"

"No—they both died about five years ago." Janey lifted her chin. "My mother ran a day-care center in our home, my father was a carpenter. That's where I learned that there's nothing wrong with working with one's hands."

"Ah," Camilla said.

The dining room would have seated twenty, but just as it had been at lunch the previous day, the table was small

enough to be comfortable for the four of them—Webb at
the head of the table, Camilla at the foot, Janey on one side
facing Maddy, in her high chair, on the other.

Janey watched as Webb carved the enormous turkey, his
hands moving surely and without hesitation as he manip-
ulated the huge knife. Maddy had inherited his hands, she
thought idly—beautiful hands, with long fingers and well-
shaped nails. She wondered when she had noticed.

She glanced down at her own hands, clasped in her lap.
There was nothing wrong with them that couldn't be fixed
by a long soak in soap and water—say for a week or two—
followed by a good manicure. Ellen had been right: it had
proved impossible to remove the remnants of engine oil
left from her last shift. And she'd broken a nail last night,
so she'd had no choice but to chop them all off short and
square. Next to the blunt-cut nails and the dark specks and
lines ingrained in her skin, Webb's enormous diamond
looked even more out of place.

Camilla cut a bite from her slice of turkey breast and
nodded at the butler as he poured her the first glass from
the dusty bottle of white wine. "I've invited some people
in for drinks on Friday evening," she said brightly.

"That's lovely, Gran," Webb murmured.

"I thought a large party wouldn't be in the best taste just
now."

The wary look that Janey was beginning to know so well
appeared once more in Webb's eyes. "The best taste for
what?"

"Your engagement *is* going to come as a surprise, you
know, to a good many people. I thought it might be better
to—in a sense—let the news trickle out," Camilla went on.
"I thought instead of an elaborate party I'd invite just a
few of our very best friends. Once they know, the word

will get around soon enough, and we can have the official announcement party a little later.''

"Gran," Webb said firmly, "I don't think we're quite ready to announce anything yet. It's going to be a long engagement—"

Camilla cut him off. "Nonsense, dear. Janey's wearing a ring, and that's a declaration all by itself. You'll be in public together—you can't hide yourselves until the wedding, no matter when it's going to be. You'll be introducing her to your friends, going out for dinner, attending parties together. We can hardly deny the obvious, and our friends would be hurt if we tried."

Janey's head was spinning. But of course it wouldn't come to that; this wasn't going to last long enough, and in the meantime she had the irrefutable excuse that she was too busy with her studies to go much of anywhere.

"You surely don't expect that she'll take her diamond off and pretend to be just a casual date when you go out, do you?" Camilla didn't wait for an answer. "However, I do think it would only be polite, Webb, if you were to tell Sibyl's parents privately before any big announcement's made."

That's her safety net, Janey thought. Camilla had built in an excuse to cancel any thought of a formal affair, for if Sibyl's parents were out of touch right now, there could be no announcement. It was almost perfect; Camilla could threaten to throw the party of the century, give Webb plenty of time to contemplate all the thousand ways the spectacle could go wrong and still never have to embarrass herself or him by actually hosting the event.

"Perhaps," Camilla added gently, "you should take Janey with you when you tell them, Webb."

The woman deserved an award, Janey thought. The very thought of being introduced to a set of parents who were no doubt still grieving as the woman who was going to replace their daughter was enough to send ice cubes through her veins—even if none of it was for real.

"At any rate," Camilla added, "I thought Friday evening would work better for our little get-together, as I'm sure you'll want to take Janey out on Saturday. There's a symphony concert that evening, and a couple of really good plays in town."

"I have a tremendous amount of studying to do this weekend," Janey said quickly.

"Nonsense." Camilla spared her no more than a glance. "You're not working tonight or tomorrow, because the plant's closed for the holiday—right?"

"Well…yes."

"And since it only operates on weekends when the work piles up, which doesn't seem to be the case right now, you won't be going back to work till Monday. So you can study when you would have been working and enjoy yourself on the weekend."

As logicians went, Janey thought, Camilla was a wonder. "I also didn't bring any clothes that are suitable."

"I suppose that really means you don't own any." Camilla sounded as if the words tasted bad.

Janey managed a smile. "That's absolutely right."

"Then we'll simply have to go shopping, won't we? You'll need a hundred things before the wedding anyway. But we can decide all that later—there's no sense in boring Webb with it. Webb, my dear, Janey's been telling me how she developed her love of buildings. Don't you think it's fascinating?"

The look Webb shot at Janey should have shriveled her in her chair. In fact, all it did was irritate her. At least she'd asked him to fill her in on the basics so she'd have a fighting chance to handle obscure questions. Webb hadn't even bothered, and now Camilla was going to nail him to the wall.

Annoyed as Janey was, though, she couldn't just abandon her partner. "It's one of the best memories I have of my father, going along with him to the construction sites he was working on."

Now if Webb didn't take a shot in the dark and refer to her father as a plumber or plasterer or ditchdigger, she thought, they might slide through.

"Couldn't you just listen to Janey's stories forever, Gran?" Webb asked. "I certainly could."

Janey relaxed a trifle. At least he'd left himself a loophole, but if his grandmother tried to pin him down…

Janey was still edgy when Camilla eventually put down her napkin and said, "Albert, you may clear. We'll have dessert and coffee in the parlor."

Janey bounced out of her chair like a jack-in-the-box. "I'm sure dessert is delightful, but I couldn't possibly do it justice right now," she announced. "Couldn't we put everything on hold for a bit till we can enjoy it more? Albert, you've worked hard and you look like a man in a hurry. Why don't you just run along and start your own holiday? Mr. Copeland and I will do the dishes."

Camilla, just starting to rise, lost her footing and fell back into her chair.

Janey leaned over Webb to give him a sideways hug that she hoped looked like spontaneous affection, and almost lost her balance. "We could stand to sort a few things out," she hissed in his ear.

"I couldn't agree more," he growled back. He steadied her as he rose. "Albert, please take Mrs. Copeland's coffee in for her, and then that'll be all."

The butler looked like a man in a daze. "Yes, sir. Whatever you wish, sir."

Janey circled the table to Maddy's high chair and lifted her out. Aside from the mashed potatoes in her hair, the child hadn't managed badly. "Come on, Maddy. Let's explore the kitchen. Do you like to do dishes?"

Camilla was on her feet again. "I doubt she's ever tried," she said tartly.

"Then it's past time to start," Janey announced. "I'm dying to see the kitchen, anyway. You know, Webb, the main flaw in Henry Bellows's floor plans for this house has to be the kitchen." As she picked up a china plate in each hand, she noticed that Camilla had paused in the doorway. "He put in all those little side rooms and pantries and cupboards that look great but are really only good for losing things in." She leaned her back against the service door to push it open. "And he'd obviously never cleared a table in his life, or he wouldn't have made anyone going from the kitchen to the dining room negotiate half a dozen turns just to get—"

She stopped dead as the service door opened and she got her first glimpse of the kitchen.

The maze of pantries Henry Bellows had designed was gone. The torturous route had disappeared. The path from dining room to kitchen was straight and wide; only a sizable butler's pantry, lined with glass doors displaying silver and china, lay between. The kitchen itself boasted all the enormous stainless-steel commercial equipment any cook could want, but splashes of color here and there—vivid copper and rich blues—made the room seem amazingly homey despite its utilitarian arrangement. It was a thousand percent improvement over the original.

Janey thought, almost in despair, *If this is an example of Sibyl's work, of Sibyl's taste…*

Of course, nothing Janey could see proved it had been Sibyl's idea, or her design. She might have had nothing to do with it. And even if it was, there was nothing for Janey to feel despairing about. She'd known coming into this scheme that she was no match for Sibyl—that she wasn't supposed to be.

But then, she hadn't expected her to be competition in Janey's own field.

Sadness washed over her—for Webb and his loss, for Maddy and the mother she'd never know. No wonder Webb was furious with his grandmother for thinking that any of a dozen women could step easily into Sibyl's place, just because they were pretty and young and knew society's rules!

Maddy was clamoring at her feet, pulling at her sweater. Janey set down the china she carried and explored drawers till she found a terry-cloth apron—so big it wrapped around the child three times, so long it had to be tied at her armpits instead of her waist. By the time she'd fixed a big bowl of barely warm suds and found a stool for Maddy to stand on, Webb had come through with a tray stacked with china and flatware.

"It's gorgeous," she said honestly. "Much more efficient."

He looked around as if he was seeing the kitchen from a whole new perspective. "Yes, but the old way was far more fun for hide-and-seek. I used to have a dozen spots where nobody'd ever found me."

"It wasn't your idea to redesign it, then?" She tried to keep her voice casual.

"It was a matter of keeping a cook, Gran said." Webb's voice was dry. "If you'd studied the question, you couldn't have come up with a better way to please her than by approving what she did to the kitchen."

At least it wasn't Sibyl. She dismissed the thought.

"Well, how was I supposed to know?" Janey said crossly. "If you'd told me—"

"How was I supposed to know you were going to start critiquing the kitchen? Are you really going to insist on washing each plate by hand?"

"It'll give us time to talk."

"So would loading the dishwasher and sitting down with a cup of coffee while it does the work. Gran won't know the difference." He put the tray down on the counter next to the sink and went back to the dining room for more.

Maddy trailed her hands through the suds in her bowl and reached for a china plate. Janey slid it away just as the soap-slick little hands touched the platinum rim. Maddy howled, and Janey grabbed some already-clean plastic measuring cups and dumped them into the bowl. Appeased, Maddy went to work.

While the hot water ran, Janey thoughtfully watched the child. When Webb came back with the last of the china, she said, without looking at him, "Maddy's not a lot like you, is she?"

"No, she's the image of her mother."

So Sibyl had been a beauty, too. *Well, you didn't expect anything else, did you?* Janey asked herself.

"So what are we talking about? I thought I handled the question of your father rather well."

"Just a little short of brilliant," Janey said dryly. "Of course it might be even better if next time you really knew what Camilla was talking about."

"How'd she find out about your father being a contractor?"

"She asked."

Webb shrugged. "So next time she asks something, tell me."

"It was just before dinner, upstairs. There wasn't time.

And just to keep the record straight, he wasn't a contractor, he was a master carpenter. When people wanted custom cabinets, complex moldings, fitted cupboards—that sort of thing—they called him.''

"And you went along and handed him nails—"

"He didn't use many. Mostly pegs, carved joints and screws.''

"I'll try to remember. Anyway, you stood by and watched, and developed a love for fine work. See? Not at all hard to deduce."

"Yeah? Well, give her a chance—she'll come up with something tougher. My head's spinning, you know.''

"From being around Gran?"

Janey nodded. "I expected her to use the cannons—I was prepared for that. You can see a cannonball coming and try to get out of its way. What I didn't anticipate was a machine gun—just as destructive and impossible to sidestep forever. Of course it's flattering, in a way—"

"How did you come up with that?"

"Because she felt it was necessary to go to that length. She must be even more afraid of me that I thought." She found a scrubbing brush and gently washed the first plate, setting it aside to drain.

Webb found a tea towel and picked up the plate to dry it. "Or more impressed.''

"Are you still on that kick?"

"You're wrong, you know. She's serious. She would never encourage Maddy to call you..."

Mother. He couldn't even get his tongue around the word, Janey noticed. It hurt him too much to think of his daughter using the term for a woman who wasn't Sibyl.

"I agree she went a little too far with that one," Janey said. "But she no doubt thinks that at this age Maddy doesn't really know what *Mama* means—she can't have memories of Sibyl, and if nobody's made a big thing of her not having a mother, she may not have realized what she's missing. Besides, I wouldn't put it past your grandmother to have set her deadline for routing me by sometime this weekend—so the whole *Mama* business would be pretty short-lived.''

"What about the party? Calling in all her friends and announcing the engagement sounds to me like she expects it to last a little longer than Monday morning.''

"Telling a few people over drinks is no worse than what you did by flashing the ring around the factory. And she carefully put off the whole idea of a big party—or didn't you notice? All you have to do is not find Sibyl's parents, because if you can't talk to them—''

"And how am I supposed to do that? I can't exactly tell Gran I've forgotten their names.''

"I suspect it won't be difficult at all. I'll bet they're off on a safari or climbing the Himalayas, and I'll lay odds that Camilla knows it.''

"They're not the type for safaris or mountain climbing.''

"So maybe they're in the Caribbean swimming with dolphins, how should I know? I don't care if they're just hanging out on a very private golf course, the point's the same. I'm betting you can't get a message to them no matter what you do, therefore—as a matter of etiquette—there can't be a formal engagement party.''

"I suppose you might be right.''

"Of course I'm right. She only said it to scare the heck out of you. She's not anxious to have the world know, anyway—just enough of it that you'll get the message on their reaction.'' She reached for another stack of china. "Though I must admit I'd like to know who she'd put on the guest list.''

Maddy slapped her bowl of soapy water with the flat

bottom of a measuring cup, and suds flew in all directions. A good-size clump ended up in Webb's eyebrow, and when Janey laughed at him he flipped it at her, hitting her almost squarely on the end of the nose. She retaliated, crowning him with a fist-size lump.

Maddy crowed with delight that they'd joined in her game, and she banged her hands into her bowl as fast as she could till it was empty. Then she tugged on Webb's sleeve, heedless of the soggy ring she left on his sweater. "More," she said.

Bits of foam decorated Maddy's dark hair, the shoulders of her bright pink dress, and the matching velvet bow atop her head. Where her apron wasn't covered with suds, it was soaked. And her smile could have lit up the city.

Janey's heart twisted, and she had to reach far back into her memory, to the days when as a teenager she'd helped her mother with the day-care kids. One small boy in particular had captivated Janey, and when he moved away she thought her heart would break. Her mother had found her mourning, and in her matter-of-fact way said, "It's hard to love them without forgetting they don't belong to you—isn't it?"

How easy it would be to get attached to Maddy. *But she doesn't belong to you,* Janey told herself. *And she never will.*

Deliberately she turned away and left Webb to deal with replenishing Maddy's water, getting the temperature just right, frothing the suds till the child was pleased and retrieving all her cups to be washed once more.

But she watched from the corner of her eye.

When Webb spoke, she hardly heard him. "In any case, it isn't necessary for you to encourage her."

"Encourage her?" Janey was bewildered. "Who— Maddy?"

"Of course not. Gran."

"What are you talking about?"

"The way you've been going overboard. You play the innocent really well, don't you? Pretending all those little smiles, those looks up through your eyelashes are accidental."

"Are you back to that again—thinking no woman could possibly take a look at you without falling flat at your feet? You're reasonably attractive, Webb, but let's face it— you're not Prince Charming. If I was in the market for a man, which I'm not, you'd be well down on my list."

"Well, you're certainly sending mixed messages about it. What about that kiss the other day? You didn't have to make it seem you were on fire to accomplish the purpose where Gran was concerned."

Janey said stiffly, "It seemed to be what you wanted. I was simply making a show of it."

"You certainly were, and not only for Gran's sake, I suspect. Talk about suggestive kisses—"

She slammed her hands into the water, much as Maddy had, with much the same result—but she paid no attention to the water that surged from the sink and splattered her sweater and slacks. "And you thought I was asking for more? I actually believed once that you couldn't possibly have a shortage of experience where women were concerned, Webb, but I was wrong on all counts. If you call *that* a suggestive kiss, you've got a lot to learn!"

He didn't say a word. He didn't have to; the quirk of his eyebrow made it obvious what he was thinking.

Janey didn't bother to dry her hands, and her fingertips were still dripping when she flung herself against him. The suddenness of the move, rather than her weight, pushed him back against the counter and she wrapped her arms around him, molding her body to his, letting her hands skim through his hair before locking at the back of his neck to pull his face down to hers.

If he wants suggestive, she thought, *I'll show him suggestive!*

She kissed him as if he was the lover of her dreams and she was supremely confident in the power of her touch. Heat—from her body? from his? she didn't know which— seemed to burn through the damp fibers of her sweater and weld them together. He tasted of the dry white wine they'd shared at dinner, but instead of a pleasant glow, this time it created a kick that went straight to her brain. She held him closer, and kissed him with lavish fervor, and let a little moan escape.

Her instinct for self-preservation warned her a split second before he turned from demonstration model to aggressor, and as his mouth grew hot against hers Janey pulled away.

"Now *that*," she said, almost too winded to speak, "was a suggestive kiss."

From the service door, Camilla, at her most acerbic, said, "It certainly was."

Janey, her face burning, cast one swift look at her and wheeled around to plunge her hands into the dishwater once more.

Camilla went on, "I felt ashamed of myself for not helping with the cleanup, so I thought I'd at least bring my cup back to the kitchen. I must admit I never realized washing dishes could be quite so…stimulating."

From the corner of her eye, Janey watched as Camilla turned on her heel and left the kitchen.

"Perfect timing," Webb said. He sounded as if he was having just a little trouble getting his breath.

"And I suppose you think I engineered that little interruption? You'll never be lonely, Webb—you've got enough ego for two. At any rate, as I was saying—*that* was a suggestive kiss. And don't forget it, because it's the last one you'll ever get from me.''

She seized the dish towel from him, dried her hands, and walked out.

CHAPTER SIX

THE hinges of the service door between the kitchen and dining room were the self-closing kind that couldn't be slammed. Good thing, too, Webb thought, or—considering the force Janey had applied to it—the door would have burst through the casing and probably taken out the far wall of the kitchen.

A little hand tugged at his sleeve. "Ma?" Maddy's face was plaintive.

That made the third time she'd said it, which for Maddy was the equivalent of giving an entire lecture series. "Her name is Janey," Webb said firmly.

Wide-eyed, Maddy took in the information, rolled it around and softly said something that—with a lot of interpretation—might have been "Janey."

"That's it," Webb congratulated. "Now you've got it."

Maddy clapped her hands in glee, and a drop of soapy water shot off her finger and straight into her eye. She howled—more in tired rage, Webb thought, than in pain—and held up her arms to him for comfort.

He untangled her from the soaked apron and cuddled her close, and with a hiccup Maddy put her head down on his shoulder and stilled.

The house was unnaturally quiet. Normally there were background noises—a vacuum running somewhere, a CD player, a soft-voiced conversation, a laugh. Today there was nothing.

He wondered if Janey had gone in search of his grandmother. If she had, he'd sign over his entire pension fund if he could listen in on the conversation.

You have enough ego for two, Janey had said. And perhaps, he admitted, there was some truth to that. But his concern for himself wasn't vanity, as she had so clearly thought. It was simple caution.

He'd been a target—both before and after his marriage—long enough to be supersensitive. And a very worthwhile target he was, too; it wasn't egotistical to admit that, just realistic. The Copeland money, social position and mansion would have been enough all by themselves—but add the fact that he was neither dull nor difficult to look at, and feminine interest soared. And now, if you factored in the challenge of bringing the grieving widower back to normal life...well, he was a package made in heaven in the eyes of a good many women.

One of the reasons he'd been so annoyed with Camilla's pageantlike parade of beauties was that the last thing he needed was his grandmother encouraging the hunt. It was plenty bad enough without her standing on the sidelines cheering the chase.

But Janey was a little different than the average, and maybe he was being unjust in suspecting her of ulterior motives. It wasn't as if she had sought him out, or created this connection herself.

On the other hand, she sure hadn't refused when it was offered, he reflected. In fact, she'd practically jumped at the chance. And he had only her word for lots of things—that she hadn't known ahead of time that he owned the Henry Bellows house of her dreams, that she hadn't deliberately let the news slip to his grandmother that she was a great deal more than a factory hand, that she hadn't changed her mind about the deal they'd agreed to and decided instead to play for much higher stakes. There was no proof she was telling the truth; he either had to accept her assurances, or not.

The only sensible thing to do was to treat Janey with the same sort of cool caution with which he handled every other female. There was still Camilla to be considered, of course, and convinced—so he couldn't precisely keep Janey at arm's length. But beyond that...

It's a shame, though, he thought. *Damn, the woman can kiss like...*

He'd almost said *an angel,* but there'd been nothing restrained, nothing cool, and certainly nothing virtuous about that kiss.

He wondered where she'd learned her technique, and wasted a couple of minutes thinking about how much fun he could have helping her perfect it.

And why not?

He recognized the little voice inside his brain that had whispered the seemingly careless question. It was the same one that had prompted him to blow an exceptionally wet spit-wad at his third-grade teacher, earning him an entire afternoon in the principal's office.

He remembered thinking, though, that the consequences had been well worth it, just to see the look on Miss Anderson's face when the spit-wad hit her squarely on the end of her nose.

What about Janey? She must have known she was courting trouble, kissing him like that. Had she done it on purpose, trying to awaken his interest in her as a woman? Hoping that he might throw out the deal they'd made and offer her a better one?

Or did it even matter what her intent had been? Whatever she'd set out to do, it didn't change the outcome. That kiss had rocked him to the toes, and he freely admitted it.

GET A FREE TEDDY BEAR...

You'll love this plush, cuddly Teddy Bear, an adorable accessory for your dressing table, bookcase or desk. Measuring 5 ½" tall, he's soft and brown and has a bright red ribbon around his neck – he's completely captivating! And he's yours *absolutely free*, when you accept this no-risk offer!

The Harlequin Reader Service® — Here's how it works:

Accepting your 2 free books and gift places you under no obligation to buy anything. You may keep the books and gift and return the shipping statement marked "cancel." If you do not cancel, about a month later we'll send you 6 additional novels and bill you just $2.90 each in the U.S., or $3.34 each in Canada, plus 25¢ delivery per book and applicable taxes if any.* That's the complete price and — compared to the cover price of $3.50 in the U.S. and $3.99 in Canada — it's quite a bargain! You may cancel at any time, but if you choose to continue, every month we'll send you 6 more books, which you may either purchase at the discount price or return to us and cancel your subscription.

*Terms and prices subject to change without notice. Sales tax applicable in N.Y. Canadian residents will be charged applicable provincial taxes and GST.

Judging by the tremor in her voice, it had done much the same to her.

So, if she was feeling the same bloom of curiosity he was, why not explore it...together?

Would the consequences be worth it?

He took Maddy up to the nursery to change her diaper, but instead of putting her in her crib for a nap he carried her back down with him, complete with teddy bear and silky blanket, all the way through the still-silent house to the television room at the far end. She could sleep there just as well as in her bed, and he'd watch football, if nobody wanted to talk to him.

As he picked up the remote control and pushed the button that elevated the big-screen television from its concealing cabinet into viewing position, Maddy raised her head from his shoulder and sleepily murmured, "Ma."

Webb swung around and saw Janey curled at the end of a long black leather couch with her shoes kicked off, a textbook open beside her, a clipboard on her lap, and an array of papers on the low cocktail table in front of her. She was obviously startled to see him.

She'd gone as far from the kitchen as she possibly could, he thought, and grinned. "Fancy that—I just followed you like a magnet."

She didn't look flattered. "You're sure it isn't the game that's the attraction, not me? I had no idea there was a television in here. I was just looking for a quiet spot to study." She leaned forward and began to shuffle papers together.

"Don't go. I don't want to make you move all that."

"And I'd rather not move it," she said frankly, "when I just got everything sorted out. So if there's another set you can use..."

"There isn't." His conscience prickled, despite the fact

that the statement was technically true. "Tell you what—if I keep the volume down, would the game bother you?"

Janey shrugged and looked at the tabletop, covered with papers. "I suppose not. I've studied through soap operas, I can no doubt study through a football game." She bent her head over the clipboard again.

He turned on the television, muted the sound and sat down at the other end of the couch. Maddy, her eyelids now barely half open, wriggled out of his arms and squirmed down the length of the couch and around the textbook, dragging her blanket, to plant herself firmly against Janey's side.

He reached for the child, but Janey shook her head. "She'll be asleep in a couple of minutes. Don't argue with her."

"I'd much rather talk to you," he agreed. "You misunderstood me, you know."

"In a dozen different ways, I'm sure." She didn't sound interested in finding out what they were.

"It's not that I seriously object to any of those things you were doing. In fact, I'd hate for you to think I didn't appreciate that little demonstration in the kitchen just now."

"Yeah? Well, my mother always told me that someday I'd regret losing my temper and acting on impulse. I had no idea how right she was."

"In fact, I don't mind if you keep right on with the flirting looks, the coy little smiles." He paused and added in a deliberate tone, "The suggestive kisses."

That made her look up, gaze wary. "I thought you didn't want me encouraging Camilla."

"She'll think what she likes anyway. There's no reason we can't have a little private fun with this. I just wanted to make it absolutely clear that I am not interested in anything permanent. So long as you realize that—"

"You'd be quite willing to let me seduce you, I suppose." Janey stared at him. "You remember what I said about the size of your ego, Webb? Well, I take it all back. It's not big enough for two, after all—it's more like triple." Her voice rose sharply; beside her, Maddy jerked in surprise and wailed. Janey set her clipboard aside and scooped the baby up into her arms. "There, there," she whispered, and Maddy relaxed again, her face nestled against Janey's breast.

"Come on, Janey. If that kiss wasn't an invitation—"

Her voice was fierce. "I was not kissing you."

"I assure you," Webb said cheerfully, "I am not *that* inexperienced. I do know a kiss when I—"

"I was making a point."

"Oh, you made it," Webb murmured.

"And as long as we're getting things clear, I want you to understand I'm not interested in you personally. You think *you* don't want anything permanent—well, the mere idea makes me shudder. In fact, the thought of seducing you makes me shudder. My only goal is the money you promised me. All right? Have we got it all straight now?"

He wondered if she really believed that she had absolutely no personal interest in him, when the explosive potential of that kiss had said something very different. Unless, of course, she was in the habit of kissing every man she knew with that same abandon? She was, after all, damnably good at it. He shook off the question. "Want to place a little bet?"

"On what?" She sounded suspicious.

"That it *won't* be the last suggestive kiss you'll ever give me?"

She didn't answer, but then he hadn't expected her to.

Lazily he rolled off the couch onto the thick carpet and stretched out on his stomach to concentrate on the game.

It was almost halftime before he realized that Janey had gone completely quiet; he hadn't even heard the rustle of a page turning in some time. Not that he needed to see her, or hear her, to know she was still there; there was the faintest aroma of her perfume in the air. Or was he smelling the portion of it that had rubbed off on him, during that incredibly physical kiss? Whatever its origin, the scent of violets tantalized his memory just as effectively as it tickled his nose.

He glanced over his shoulder. Janey had slumped down into the most uncomfortable-looking position he'd ever seen. Her eyes were closed, one foot dangled off the couch and a sound-asleep Maddy was sprawled across her body, held safely close despite Janey's own state of unconsciousness.

If she spent much longer in that position, he thought, she'd never be able to stand up straight again. He eased the open textbook out from under Maddy's feet and put it on the table. The clipboard was more difficult; Janey's elbow was resting heavily on it. As he pulled it free, she shifted and muttered, and he stood patiently, reading the essay she'd been drafting, while he waited for her to settle once more so he could try turning her into a more comfortable position.

Her eyelids fluttered as he moved her, and he looked down into her eyes. The green-flecked hazel depths made him think of forest pools, deep and still and full of mystery.

She raised her hand as if to touch his face, but she seemed to lack muscle control and it fell back to the couch. The first completely natural smile he had ever seen on her face flickered into life. For once she wasn't trying to impress Camilla, she wasn't shooting ironic darts at him. She was simply smiling.

Except there was nothing simple about it. She was half innocent, half seductive—and altogether tempting.

With a feather light touch he smoothed the hair back from her temple and leaned closer till his breath brushed her cheek and his lips were just millimeters from hers.

Down the hall, the telephone rang sharply. Janey's eyes opened wide. Webb couldn't decide if he was more annoyed by the interruption or amused by the comprehension that flooded into her face. Prudence made him draw back just as Janey raised her hand again, because this time, he thought, it wasn't a caress she had in mind.

He had to admit he deserved it. Sneaking around trying to steal kisses from a sleeping woman...from *Janey*... What was wrong with him, anyway? Didn't he have anything better to do?

She'd been dreaming, Janey knew that—though she hadn't dreamed his face, mere inches away as she opened her eyes. But had she dreamed the touch of his fingers, the whisper of a kiss?

She couldn't decide which would be worse. If she'd created those caresses in her mind, there was something distinctly amiss in her subconscious and the sooner it was sorted out the better. But if she hadn't imagined it, then it had really happened. And if he had actually pressed that ghost of a kiss on her...

Her lips were tingling. But was that reaction, or warning?

Webb, she thought irritably, would probably say it was anticipation!

She lay still, stretched out on her back and almost pinned in place by Maddy's weight. She was trying to shift the child aside so she could sit up, knowing she'd be much more comfortable facing him that way than sprawled on the couch, when Webb reappeared. As efficiently as if she'd been a rag doll, he lifted Maddy and rearranged her at the opposite end of the couch.

Once free, Janey sat up straight and eyed with caution the way his jaw was set. "Bad news?"

"I'm sure Gran won't think so. But then, since she probably arranged it, that shouldn't come as any surprise."

Janey sighed. "What now?"

"Oh, she's really done it this time," Webb said grimly.

As if the mere mention had summoned her, Camilla's step sounded in the hallway.

"That was Mrs. Wilson's sister," Webb said as Camilla came in, "calling to tell me she's not coming back to work tonight. Or probably tomorrow, for that matter."

Camilla's eyes sparkled. "Do you mean she's quit? Now that's something to be thankful for. I've *never* liked—"

"No, Gran." His gaze met Janey's and she could almost read his mind. If Camilla had arranged this scene, she wouldn't admit even under torture that she knew precisely what he was talking about. "Her sister says she's picked up some sort of a bug and she's so sick we shouldn't count on her for at least a couple of days."

Camilla nodded briskly. "Undercooked turkey, I imagine. I'm sure she'll be fine by Saturday."

"And just how do you know when she'll be well?" Webb's voice dripped irony.

Camilla looked vaguely surprised. "I don't, dear. It was just a feeling, and now that I really stop to think about it, I can't imagine any turkey having enough nerve to poison Mrs. Wilson. So it's probably something contagious instead." Her tone grew brisk. "And of course you're right, we should take no chances of her coming back too soon and giving it to Maddy. I suppose you told her to take the whole week off, just to be certain?''

Janey's jaw had gone slack. Webb looked as if he'd been hit by a brick—and no wonder, Janey thought. In a matter of seconds, Camilla had reversed the whole situation, given Webb credit for powers that verged on the psychic and—by picturing him as a hero for putting his daughter's health above everything else—made it impossible for him to argue otherwise without sounding like a fool.

"No," Webb said dryly. "I thought I'd leave that one to you. Perhaps you should call her right now and relieve her mind."

Camilla was imperturbable. "Tomorrow will be early enough. She might miraculously heal after all."

Janey could almost read Webb's mind. *Not unless you tell her to,* he wanted to say.

Camilla sat down in an overstuffed chair. "Do you play bridge, Janey?"

"No, I'm sorry. I've never learned."

"Oh, that's all right. I'm afraid three-handed isn't my favorite, anyway, but I thought you might enjoy a break from studying." She eyed the papers spread across the cocktail table. "Though of course tomorrow will be pretty much of a break, won't it? If we're going shopping, and out for lunch..." She paused. "Webb, my dear, do you have a very busy day tomorrow?"

"Yes. So if you were going to suggest that I take Maddy to work with me—"

Janey was puzzled. "I thought you'd declared an extra holiday."

"I did," Webb said. "For everyone but me. It'll be nice and quiet, and I can catch up with my paperwork in peace."

"Of course I didn't mean you should take her all day,"

Camilla murmured. "I just thought, since I've made reservations, that perhaps for an hour or so..."

"I'm meeting a supplier for lunch."

Camilla acquiesced, with a smile. "Very well. We'll just consider it a perfect opportunity for Maddy and Janey to get to know each other—and for Maddy to practice her manners in public." She stood up. "Would anyone besides me like dessert now? Since you two did the dishes, I'll take my turn and serve it up."

She strolled out without waiting for an answer.

Webb sat down on the arm of the couch next to Janey.

"You really think she arranged for Mrs. Wilson to get sick?" Janey asked.

"You're the one who gives her credit for being Machiavelli. But it does seem just a little too convenient."

"Well...yes. I imagine she wants to judge for herself what kind of parent I'd make. I wonder what the best way will be to disillusion her."

"You could spank Maddy in public, I suppose."

Janey's gaze flicked to the child, flushed cheek pressed against the soft leather, dark hair curling around her ears, looking perfectly angelic—and tried to imagine spanking her. Perhaps if the child was to do something truly dangerous? "No, I couldn't. I guess I'll just have to ignore her as much as possible. If I look like I don't want to be bothered with the baby when you're not around to see how maternal I am..."

She thought Webb looked relieved, and wondered if it was because he didn't believe in spanking or because he didn't want Maddy to get attached to Janey any more than she wanted to fall in love with the child.

"There's a good side, though," she offered. "It's a great excuse to keep Camilla's little get-together Friday evening from getting out of hand."

"Why?"

"Just hint that you think Maddy's already coming down with Mrs. Wilson's bug. Really, Webb—don't you think her face looks a little feverish right now?"

"She always looks that rosy when she sleeps."

"I'm very glad to hear it. But all you have to do is hint, you know. Camilla wouldn't want to risk having Maddy get sick in the midst of her special evening, because without a nurse to take care of her it would break up the party. And she can't deny the possibility without admitting that Mrs. Wilson's bug is a fraud."

Webb looked at her thoughtfully. "Janey, you're almost as twisted as Gran is."

"Thanks, I think. But at least it means you don't have to rely on Sibyl's parents for an excuse to keep things quiet. Actually I'm still betting they're sailing the South Pacific, but just in case they took a cell phone along—"

"Impossible."

"They don't believe in cell phones?"

"She gets seasick. Wherever they are, it's not on a sailboat." He grinned. "You know, it's almost a temptation to call, just to see whether you're right."

Janey hoped he wouldn't. She thought that they were pushing their luck as it was.

Camilla had told her, as they retired, that Janey should sleep as late as she wanted because Albert would arrange for her breakfast at any hour. She herself would be downstairs promptly at eight, Camilla added.

Janey, who didn't have to be hit over the head with a hint, filed that fact in her mental alarm clock, and it was just a couple of minutes past eight when she came into the sunny little gallery at the back of the house where Camilla had said breakfast was always served.

With its wide windows, big potted plants, casual glass-topped round table and checkerboard parquet floor, the room had the feeling of a gazebo. It was unexpectedly bright and cheery for a late November day, and Janey paused for a moment to take it all in before she walked around the table to the empty seat beside Maddy's high chair. She rubbed her knuckles gently on the top of the child's head—the only spot she could see that was still pristine—and said, "Hello, squirt. I always thought the oat-meal was supposed to go on the inside. Unless you really think you're old enough for facials?"

Maddy grinned and banged her spoon on the high chair's tray.

Camilla had a coffee cup and a notebook in front of her, and as Janey sat down she jotted another phrase and pushed the book aside. She looked just a little askance at Janey's favorite faded jeans, but she said a calm good-morning and rang the small bell beside her plate to summon the butler. Then she looked across the table. "Webb, you may recall that a gentleman stands when a lady comes into the room."

"Hi, Janey." Webb half rose from his place, but he hardly took his eyes off the newspaper.

Janey raised her eyebrows and turned to Camilla. "Is there something incredible in the news today, or is he always like this in the morning?"

"Always," Webb said without looking up.

"It's just a bad habit he's gotten into," Camilla said. "I'm sure you can cure him of it, Janey."

A bad habit. Janey wondered just when he'd acquired it, and why. Breakfast might well be one of the worst times of the day for him, one of the strongest memories. It was certainly the time when he and Sibyl would have been least likely to be interrupted by business or telephones or visitors. Had he taken to reading the paper at the breakfast table because it helped him forget Sibyl's empty chair?

Empty no longer, of course; it must be that chair that Janey was now occupying. She wondered which was worse for him—seeing the silent reminder of the hole in his life, or looking across the table at a woman who was only pretending to fill the gap. No wonder he didn't want to take his nose out of the paper to make polite conversation.

The sadness that welled up in her drowned her appetite. Why couldn't Camilla see that this man was in no way ready to love again? Or did she know it and simply not care? Or perhaps, knowing there would never be another love for Webb, she had presented the alternative of a sensible marriage? Were all the beauties she'd paraded before him willing to accept an alliance rather than a romance?

Janey found it a little hard to believe that their standards were all so low that they'd settle for a loveless marriage. And yet—it was Webb they were talking about. To have Webb, a woman might compromise on a lot of other things…

Some women, she clarified, might want him that badly. She could understand the feeling in the abstract, even though it had no personal significance.

She realized that Albert was asking for her breakfast order for at least the second time. "Just toast and coffee," she said. "Thanks, Albert."

"It'll be a busy day," Camilla said pointedly. "It takes energy to shop."

Janey watched as Albert poured coffee into her cup. "I was just thinking about that," she began. "There's really no need for us to shop. Since we won't be going out on Saturday—"

"Why on earth not?" Camilla sounded puzzled.

"If Mrs. Wilson won't be back—well, we can hardly leave Maddy."

"Nonsense. Do you really think I've forgotten how to give a child a bath? I may be old, but I'm not archaic." Camilla's smile was just short of sly. "Besides, if Webb makes your reservations fashionably late, all that can be done before you go. Then all I'll need to do is carry the baby monitor around and listen to her sleep."

Janey felt as if she'd been boxed, wrapped and tied up with string before she'd even been able to open her mouth to object.

"And you'll still need something to wear tonight," Camilla said comfortably.

Now was the time, Janey thought, to try out the suggestion that Maddy didn't look well enough for a party. Except nobody in their right minds could look at the child—bright-eyed, happy, enthusiastically coated in oatmeal—and say that she appeared anything but excruciatingly healthy.

Webb seemed to have reached the same conclusion, for he simply shrugged.

Camilla added cheerfully, "And you haven't forgotten the need to get in touch with Sibyl's parents, have you, Webb? The sooner the better, you know—I'd hate to have them hear via the grapevine." She tore the top page out of her notebook and pushed it across the table to Janey. "I've made a minimal list of what we'll need to look for today."

Janey didn't bother to read the individual entries; the sheer length of the list was enough to make her stomach feel as empty as her wallet.

Webb folded his newspaper and stood up. "How much cash do you think you'll need, Janey?" He pulled a money clip from his pocket.

"Don't be ridiculous," Camilla said. "You can't buy Janey clothes before the wedding, it's not proper. Of course, if you'd like to find her a car as an engagement gift—"

"Is that a hint that you'd like me to leave mine for you to use today?"

"No, thanks," Janey said firmly. Get behind the wheel of Webb's car and be responsible for it? Maybe when the sun turned green.

Camilla eyed her with interest. "Actually, on this kind of trip I prefer to take cabs. Then someone else can worry about parking." She held up her cheek for Webb to kiss.

He walked around the table and rubbed enough oatmeal off Maddy's forehead to leave room for a kiss, then leaned over Janey's chair. "Don't get up," he said. "You'll only distract me."

His voice was husky for Camilla's benefit, Janey told herself. And the de rigueur kiss would be as well. She braced herself to sit primly and not respond; she'd show him she meant what she'd said where suggestive kisses were concerned.

His mouth moved over hers—gentle, slow, tormentingly thorough. His teeth nipped softly at her lower lip in a lover's bite. It took every bit of Janey's self-control to stay still, and Webb knew it—that was obvious from the laughter in his eyes as he straightened up once more.

She'd told him yesterday that she regretted losing her temper and acting on impulse by kissing him—but only now did she begin to realize how much trouble she'd bought herself with that rash action. He could kiss her anytime he wanted, as long as he had a suitable audience—and all she could do was let him.

Camilla waited until the sound of his footsteps had faded before she pushed her cup aside. "I thought we'd start—after you finish your toast and we soak the oatmeal off Madeline—by looking in at the master bedroom. That way you can start thinking about what you'll want to do there. And if we're lucky enough about finding clothes, perhaps there'll be time today to stop at the decorating salon as well.''

Janey stared at the half slice of toast in her hand. Maybe it was crazy, but she found herself starting to wonder precisely why Webb was so opposed to the idea of a nice, sane, mutual-advantage, loveless marriage. No wife—and especially one who didn't even pretend to be romantically involved—could possibly be as set on organizing his life as Camilla was!

Or was it just Janey she was organizing? Perhaps because she felt someone had to and Janey herself wasn't capable? Or was she nagging—politely, gently, but indubitably nagging—in an attempt to drive Janey into some angry, inappropriate response?

I'll just have to make sure Webb sees it, she thought. *It would be the perfect ending to this incredible scam.*

An hour later, she was approaching the master suite with trepidation, torn between raging curiosity and reluctance to invade Webb's privacy. Camilla seemed to show no such hesitation; she pushed open the suite's main door and swept down the long hall with assurance. Janey, with Maddy toddling beside her and holding fast to her hand, trailed behind.

Camilla threw open the door at the end of the hallway and stepped aside to let Janey look in.

Sunlight flooded through windows on three sides of the room, which occupied the entire end of the wing, and sparkled against peach satin drapes, peach plush carpet, peach silk bedspread, peach lace peignoir laid across a peach tapestry chaise longue. At first glance it seemed everything but the marble mantel was peach…and ruffled.

If the room hadn't been huge, the ambiance would have

been overwhelming, but the fairy-princess decor stopped—
in Janey's opinion—just a couple of inches short of ludi-
crous.

"Oh, my," she said. It was all she could manage.

Over the mantel was an oil portrait of one of the most
striking women Janey had ever seen. It was unmistakably
Sibyl, for the huge dark eyes were just like Maddy's, and
even the shape of her face was the same, although with
fashionably hollow cheeks instead of Maddy's chubby
ones.

A portrait of her over the mantel...her peignoir still lying
across the chaise. *The place is nothing short of a shrine.*

No wonder Camilla had been so insistent she see this.
She was covering all her bases. There was no clearer way
to point out that the practical Janey was just about as far
from the romantic Sibyl as it was possible to get. Nobody
could have missed that message.

Janey hardly knew she was speaking. "How can anyone
compete with a woman like this?"

"Personally," Camilla said, "I'd suggest you not try."

Stunned, hardly believing what she'd heard, Janey
wheeled around to stare at her.

There was no sarcasm in Camilla's voice; her tone was
perfectly conversational. She wasn't trying to make a point,
Janey realized—she was simply stating a fact.

It was even a fact that Janey happened to agree with—
and confirmation that their plan was working. They'd
wanted Camilla to find Janey unacceptable, and they'd certainly been successful.

So why, Janey asked herself, should that simple statement of Camilla's feel like a hard slap across the face?

CHAPTER SEVEN

JANEY was still reeling in shock when Camilla went on. In fact, there'd been only a momentary pause, just long enough to let the statement sink in and her meaning become clear. "I meant, of course, that you're very different—and perhaps the contrast is part of the reason Webb finds you so attractive."

That cut uncomfortably close to the bone. Even if Janey had wanted to pursue the subject, she knew it was a great deal safer to get on to something else before Camilla had a chance to contemplate the possibility that the clashing differences between Janey and Sibyl had been the entire reason for Webb's choice, not just part of it.

She almost tiptoed across the deep carpet. In the fireplace, logs were laid and kindling was in place for a romantic fire that had never been lit. Flanking the mantel were two huge armoires, matching pieces that had been painted peach. "I hope these weren't antiques," she said under her breath, running her fingertips over the smooth surface.

Under her hand, a pressure latch released and the door popped open. Inside the armoire was a television set almost as large as the one downstairs.

"So much for his not being able to watch the game anywhere but downstairs," Janey said.

"Did he tell you that?" Camilla sounded intrigued. "I imagine he didn't feel like being alone."

And any company would be better than none. Camilla might as well come straight out and say it, Janey thought.

"Though I'm not certain whether he's had this one fixed yet," Camilla went on thoughtfully. "At one time it was—shall we say?—the object of some frustration."

And just how long ago was that? Janey wanted to ask. But it wasn't any concern of hers. No doubt Webb still, from time to time, felt like beating on something. In fact, as Maddy grew, his frustration and sense of loss might get even worse in some ways—not only for his own sake but for the child who would never know her mother.

She closed the armoire door and moved on across the room.

"The dressing room and bath are through there," Camilla said pointedly.

"Both peach, no doubt?" It was a throwaway question—but at least, Janey was happy to see, the fixtures Henry Bellows had chosen remained in place. The claw-foot tub was now wearing a ruffled peach skirt so frivolous she wanted to rip it to shreds, but there had been no structural changes—nothing at all that couldn't be reversed.

Not that it was likely to be changed anytime soon, Janey reminded herself. And she didn't have any great desire for the job, anyway. But if Webb ever did give in to his grandmother's persuasion and marry one of her parade of sensible beauties, the new Mrs. Copeland would certainly want to put her own spin on that bedroom. On the other hand, without a strong romantic attachment to his new bride, Webb would likely feel equally strongly about maintaining the shrine.

And I, Janey thought, *would positively enjoy listening in on that fight!* "You've given me some things to think about."

"I hoped so," Camilla murmured.

"But I think for right now I've seen enough." Janey skirted the enormous bed, trying not to notice the peach velvet headboard. Trying not to imagine Webb amidst the ruffles and lace and satin.

The average man, she thought, would look merely silly surrounded by this ocean of femininity. She suspected, however, that Webb would be the exception—and the intense masculinity he projected so effortlessly could well be enough to make the whole confection look charming rather than cloyingly sweet. Webb, half lying in that pile of decorative pillows, would be the one contrasting note that drew all attention to him. Webb, smiling and teasing…

Webb and Sibyl.

You weren't going to think about that, she reminded herself.

Just as Janey reached the door, Maddy dropped the high-heeled slipper she'd dug from under the chaise longue, held out her arms and began to shriek.

Janey looked over her shoulder. "I'm right here, Maddy," she stated reasonably. "And your grandma is right behind you. We're not deserting you."

Maddy scrambled toward her, and Janey retraced her steps and picked up the child. Maddy promptly stopped imitating a siren and grinned, showing off teeth that gleamed just as brightly as the tears that were still rolling down her cheeks.

So much for keeping my distance, Janey thought, *and showing no particular interest in her.*

"You're right, we should go down." Camilla checked her wristwatch. "The cab should be here any time, and I want to get an early start. We have so much to do."

At the bottom of the stairs, Janey stopped abruptly. "What about Maddy's car seat? She can't ride without one, but what are we going to do with it between cab rides?"

"I'm certainly not dragging a safety seat from store to store," Camilla said firmly, "any more than I plan to carry all my packages. That's why, when I have serious shopping to do, I always hire the cab for all day.''

It was a luxury that would never have occurred to Janey. "It's apparent I'm from the peasant class," she muttered.

The day after the Thanksgiving holiday was traditionally the busiest shopping day of the year and the official kickoff for the Christmas season. Everyone in Chicago, it seemed, had gone shopping. Streets were clogged with vehicles, and pedestrians surged from the sidewalks without concern for traffic patterns. Shopping bags and boxes were too numerous to count—so many that Janey wondered how people managed to keep track of them all. Camilla's cab was looking like a better idea by the minute.

But when the cab finally forced its way through the maze on the Magnificent Mile to a nearby side street and pulled over, Camilla led the way to a narrow little storefront that looked almost abandoned.

Inside, Janey took one look around and knew why the place seemed to have no customers. It didn't even look like a shop, but like a formal parlor. The only hint of its real function was a single dress—a slim swath of gold lamé—displayed and subtly spotlighted on a platform at one side of the room, looking more like a sculpture than a fashion design.

That single dress probably cost more, Janey thought, than all the clothes she'd ever worn in her life put together. Including her diapers.

She stopped the instant Maddy's stroller was clear of the door. Camilla might mean well by bringing her to a favorite shop, without even pausing to consider the cost. Or she might have intended this as one more step in convincing Janey that she didn't belong in Webb's life. The motivation really didn't matter, of course; the point was that Janey couldn't afford a deep breath of this rarified atmosphere, much less a garment.

With a tinge of regret, she remembered Webb pulling out his money clip, offering her cash. Even if Camilla hadn't objected to the propriety of the gesture, Janey wouldn't have taken the money—it would just be one more sum to eventually pay back. Nevertheless, it would have been so pleasant, for once, to have enough cash in her pocket that she didn't feel like a fraud even to walk into a place like this.

Of course, after she'd looked her fill here, she'd have taken the cash to the nearest discount department store, where it would go ten times as far...

"I can't afford the price tags," she muttered.

"Perhaps the clothes aren't as pricey as you think."

"I wasn't talking about the *clothes*," Janey said. "I mean I probably don't have enough money to buy one of the paper labels."

Camilla actually laughed at that. Janey was fascinated at how genuine amusement lit up the woman's face.

"I can hardly buy you pots and pans for Christmas," Camilla said. "Even if you were going to need them, it wouldn't be very much fun. And gifts should be frivolous, don't you think? So why not a dress? A beautiful and totally impractical dress?"

Janey looked at the gold lamé gown. It must be only her imagination, but the reflections on the shiny fabric looked like dollar signs. "If what you have in mind is that impractical, maybe we could just rent it?" she asked wryly.

Maddy leaned out of her stroller to tug at Janey's jacket and pointed at the gold dress. "Pretty," she announced.

Feeling as if she'd been ganged up on, Janey surrendered.

*   *   *

Webb and the supplier he was meeting for lunch snagged the last table at Coq Au Vin. Webb thought they'd managed the feat not so much because the maître d' recognized him as a regular customer, but because of the denomination of the bank note in Jack Baxter's hand.

Despite the restaurant's usually dignified atmosphere, the dining room was noisy today, filled with laughter and excited chatter and even a child's shrill voice calling, "Daddy!" Who, Webb wondered, had dared bring a small child to a place like this? Even Camilla, who seldom went to any restaurant except Coq au Vin, surely had changed her reservation when she realized Maddy would be in the party...hadn't she?

He paused with his hand on the back of his chair and looked, just in case—and four tables away he spotted his daughter's dark eyes peering over the back of a high chair that she was doing her best to upset. He would never have dreamed that Coq Au Vin owned such a thing.

He sighed. Maddy might be just past a year old, but when she decided not to be ignored, she could summon up the lung power of the entire Mormon Tabernacle Choir. And once she'd seen him...

"Sorry, Jack," he said. "It looks as if I need to make a small detour. My daughter, the future spy, has detected me." Without waiting for an answer, he maneuvered past a waiter and two busboys to reach Camilla's table.

Maddy reached up to him, eyes pleading for rescue.

"Don't give me that look," he said. "I doubt very much that you're being tortured, and I'm certain you'll have more fun shopping this afternoon than you would in my office—where you would absolutely have to take a nap."

Maddy appeared to be thinking it over.

Jack appeared at Webb's elbow. "I really must be introduced."

His gaze, Webb noted, was fixed on Janey, and his eyes had practically glazed. "Ladies, this is Jack Baxter. Jack, my grandmother, Camilla Copeland. My daughter, Madeline. And this is Janey Griffin." Webb paused, deliberately. "My fiancée."

Jack blinked. "Your..."

"Very nice to meet you," Camilla said. "Webb, I believe your waiter is hovering—and about to give your table away. Janey, are you ready to go? Madeline apparently is."

Webb untangled Maddy from the high chair and handed her to Janey. "How's it going?" He thought Janey looked a little glazed herself—though not as bad as Jack, who was standing there like a lump just staring at her. "I don't see any packages."

"She's already sent the cab home to unload once. Webb, you could have warned me that where shopping's concerned, your grandmother takes no prisoners. Is there some Visigoth blood there somewhere? Genghis Khan was her direct ancestor?"

He laughed and kissed her cheek. "She can't keep up the pace for nearly as long these days."

"This is supposed to comfort me? See you tonight—if I survive." She smiled over his shoulder at Jack and hurried after Camilla.

Jack was still a bit glassy-eyed when they sat down. Webb didn't blame him, exactly; without any warning the man had been exposed to the full effect of Janey in close-fitting jeans. On the factory floor she'd been distracting enough in that costume, but here the contrast with every other woman in the restaurant made her stand out a mile. Jack clearly had no hint that she was dressed that way because she didn't have anything else to wear. Webb found it almost humorous that in the elegant surroundings of Coq Au Vin, Janey in jeans looked slightly eccentric, self-assured enough to wear what she liked and damn the conventions, and sexy as hell.

With his daughter in her arms, she looked…

Quit while you're ahead, he warned himself. *There's no sense in borrowing trouble.*

Preparations for Camilla's party were well under way when Webb got home, and the entire main floor buzzed with activity. Upstairs, however, was a different story. Camilla's bedroom door was closed, as was Janey's, and the nursery was silent and empty.

He tapped gently at Janey's door, and wondered, when there was no answer, whether they might still be out shopping. Surely not, with a party starting in a couple of hours.

The door opened a crack, letting him see only a slice of Janey's face. "I almost didn't hear you knock," she said.

"I didn't want Gran to hear. Can I talk to you a minute before the party?"

She looked at him in silence for a long moment. "You'd better come in."

Her toes were all that peeked out from under the hem of a white terry robe that would have passed muster in a convent, but as she stepped back from the door, Webb got a glimpse of a long slim bare leg. It was a view made even more enticing by the fact that everything else was left to his imagination; was she wearing anything at all under that bulky robe?

"Wouldn't you know it," he said. "When I finally get asked into your bedroom, there isn't time to take full advantage of the invitation."

"Don't get any bright ideas," Janey warned, "because—"

An infuriated shriek sounded from the bathroom. "Ma!"

"Maddy's in the tub," Janey went on unnecessarily.

"Otherwise my bathroom is the last place I'd choose to have a conference."

Almost briskly she led the way across the room. He glanced at the dress spread out across the bed and was half-disappointed; it was dull moss green and very plain, with a high neck and long sleeves and nothing more than a few cutouts around the throat and shoulders to add a little interest. Had it been Janey's choice, he wondered, or Camilla's?

"There's a perfectly good bathtub in the nursery," he stated.

Janey wrinkled her nose. "Have you ever noticed that place is practically sterile? Besides, we were running very late, and it seemed easier to bring Maddy in here than it was to move all my things. At least this way I can get ready for the party while she plays."

Webb grinned. "Don't let me change your plans."

Janey didn't even hesitate. "Honest? You really don't mind watching me brush my teeth and gargle? What's up, anyway?"

Webb sat down on the edge of the tub, and Maddy pushed a plastic boat at him. "I thought you were going to ignore her."

"I've tried." He thought she sounded a little defensive. "With just about as much success as you had at the restaurant today."

"Ouch."

"Well, I just wanted you to know it wasn't my idea for her to take a fancy to me. She's here now because your grandmother was worn-out by the time we got home, and everybody else was busy with the party."

Maddy splashed merrily, flooding her toy boat and making noises that might have been intended as foghorns, whistles and outboard engines.

Janey picked up an eye shadow brush. "So what did you want to tell me?"

"Just that I couldn't reach the Herringtons." She looked a bit perplexed, and he amplified, "Sibyl's parents."

"I told you so."

"But I left a message with the maid."

Maddy abruptly tired of the bath and demanded to get out. Webb wrapped her in a big towel and held her on his lap.

Janey's eye shadow brush was still hanging in mid-air. "You didn't actually tell the maid, did you?"

"Of course not—I just asked for the Herringtons to call me when they get back." He gently rubbed Maddy's hair with the end of the towel.

"I wonder where they are."

"She's too well trained to say."

Janey ran the brush over one eyelid. "At least that puts the clamps on Camilla's announcement for the duration— not that it's any surprise."

He stood Maddy on the counter and took the hair dryer from its mounting on the wall. "Gran's right, though, about this not being the kind of secret that keeps well. It's a little late to try putting the genie back in the bottle when I've been introducing you to my suppliers at public restaurants. So I think we'll just have to brace ourselves for some kind of recognition tonight."

Janey put out her hand. "Here, give me that hair dryer— the way you're going, the child will look like she saw a spook on Halloween and hasn't recovered yet." She smoothed Maddy's hair into a shining dark cap and added thoughtfully, "You didn't have to introduce me. You could have just told him I was a friend of the family."

"And stood there while he drooled all over you and

asked you for a date, I suppose—and then explained *that* to Gran.''

"Do you think he would have?" She looked intrigued.

Webb was a bit annoyed. Had she been as blinded by that first encounter as Jack obviously had? "Look, if you're still interested in Jack Baxter when this is done with, I'll introduce you all over again."

A slow smile lit her face, and for a moment he thought she was going to laugh at her own silliness. That was a relief; the idea of her going gaga over Jack Baxter, of all people—

Instead she said, "Thanks, Webb, you're a real pal. I'll remember that. Now are you going to get Maddy dressed for the party, or shall I?"

His grandmother was already in the parlor when Webb came down the stairs very slowly and patiently, because Maddy insisted on descending by herself, sitting on each step and scooting down to the next, so proud of her accomplishment she could hardly contain herself.

Camilla exclaimed over the child's new powder blue velvet and white lace dress and straightened the elaborate matching bow in her hair. "Didn't we do well on our shopping trip today?" The question was directed at Webb as much as at Maddy, and obviously Camilla didn't expect an answer.

"Personally," Webb said, "I think the results were mixed." He handed Camilla a sherry glass. "What inspired you to let her buy that dress?"

Camilla blinked in surprise, then her gaze rested on Maddy. "You don't like the pale blue velvet? I admit she's even prettier in darker colors, but she seemed to like this one so well—"

"I meant Janey."

Camilla sounded puzzled. "But I thought surely..." She looked over his shoulder toward the hall.

Webb turned around and caught his breath at the sight of Janey descending the winding stairway.

The dress that had looked so plain, so shapeless, lying across her bed was a whole different story once she'd put it on. The moss green velvet was shaped into a soft silhouette that skimmed rather than hugged Janey's curves. The skirt wasn't unreasonably short, though it still managed—perhaps assisted by the graceful staircase—to show off those incredible legs. And the color wasn't nearly as muted as it had looked upstairs—it made her eyes look sea green instead of their normal hazel.

The cut out patches he'd noted at the throat and shoulders of the dress—the ones that had looked so innocuous against the high-cut collar and long sleeves—now showed themselves in their true light. They were larger, more numerous, and far more revealing than they'd first appeared, leaving in effect only a few velvet straps to form the neck and shoulders of the dress. The high collar was really only a band connecting the straps; Janey's throat was nearly bare and the neckline plunged farther than he would have thought possible. The velvet sleeves extended all the way to the wrists, but the top of them was only a network of narrow velvet bands that left her shoulders bare as well.

The contrast between the virginal shape of the dress and the wicked reality actually made it far more tantalizing than if it had been entirely strapless.

He was glad Jack Baxter wasn't here to see this. If Janey in jeans had left him speechless, this spectacle would have turned him into a babbling idiot.

"You don't find it attractive?" Camilla asked innocently.

Webb was still trying to get his breath back. "All I want to know is who picked it out," he said.

"Do you mean it isn't apparent? Madeline, of course. Though I think she was more interested in the texture than the style—she seemed to like the gold lamé even better than this, until it scratched her."

Maddy had toddled out to the hallway and was standing beside Janey, her cheek nestled into the soft velvet skirt and Janey's hand resting softly atop her head, when the doorbell rang to announce the first of the two dozen guests. Webb saw Janey square her shoulders and take a deep breath as Albert crossed the hall to answer the door.

"Don't fret," he murmured. "Everybody will be too busy staring at the dress to give a thought to who's inside it."

"No doubt that's why Camilla chose it," she whispered back, and a moment later the guests were upon them.

It was more than an hour before there was a chance for another private word; Webb was sipping a drink and considering the range of hors d'oeuvres when Janey came up beside him.

"Apparently everybody knows," she said. "But even though everybody's looking at the ring, nobody's made a comment about it. Camilla must have whispered it in confidence."

"Whatever she did, it won't stay quiet. About that dress," he said. "Did Gran really choose it?"

"You don't think this was my idea, do you? It was the middle of the afternoon, I was dead on my feet, Maddy had given up and gone to sleep in her stroller and your grandmother was still going strong. I was too tired to argue." She selected a tiny seafood-filled puff pastry and put it on her plate. "So how many of the women here tonight are your old flames, Webb?"

"Not as many as there are men who'd like to be your new one."

She waved a dismissive hand. "That's not me, that's the dress—you said so yourself. Tell me how many of your girlfriends are here, and I'll tell you who they are." She tipped her head back and looked up at him.

The saucy glint in her eyes made him say, "Bet you can't. There are three."

"Only three? I expected at least six—after a day of shopping with her, I thought Camilla's specialty was overkill." She thoughtfully speared a spicy meatball. "The blonde with the martini glass, and the tiny lady with the very short hair and the dimples. They're conferring in the corner of the hall right now."

He looked over his shoulder and nodded. "Not bad."

"Well, they were obvious. For the third one..." She took a step back and looked him over as if she'd never seen him before, and then let her gaze sweep across the party guests. "I'll say the statuesque brunette who's flirting with the military guy."

He was impressed despite himself. "You should have made the bet."

"Wouldn't have been fair to you. What gave them away was the way they looked at me when they saw the diamond. Are you certain that's all of them?"

Webb almost inhaled an ice cube. "Whose dating history are we talking about here? If *I* don't know how many—"

"Because I'd have bet on the redhead Camilla's recruiting for her bridge table, too. She gave me the same look."

"Oh, her. She wasn't really a girlfriend."

"Not *really?*" She smiled. "I thought so."

As she spun away, he reached out for her arm. "Wait a minute—where are you going?"

"To hear what they have to say about you and me, of

course. Camilla would be very unhappy if I didn't take the opportunity to find out how ridiculous they think this engagement is.''

Behind him, the butler spoke. ''I'm sorry to disturb you for a telephone call, sir—but Mr. Herrington said it was quite important that he speak to you.''

The laughter died out of Janey's eyes. Webb put down his plate of tidbits and went out to answer the phone.

He was gone a long time, and Janey was aware of every second of it. Camilla organized her bridge tables and the players retreated to concentrate on the cards. Janey listened to two cute anecdotes about Webb and several slightly malicious comments about her from the former girlfriends. Maddy, frustrated at a square peg that wouldn't fit in the round hole she'd selected for it, stamped her foot and screamed. Janey, glad of the excuse, picked her up and retreated to the library, just off the parlor, to sit by the fire and rock her.

From her chair she could see most of the party, but because the library was only dimly lighted the guests had a harder time seeing her. Perhaps, she thought, that was why Webb didn't seek her out when he reappeared—he might not even have seen her. He joined a group of guests instead, laughing and talking. But, was it only her imagination, or was his laughter a little forced, his face a bit preoccupied?

Camilla's bridge game broke up, and soon afterward so did the party. The moment the last guest was gone, Camilla lifted the sleeping Maddy from Janey's arms and took her up to the nursery. ''And then I'm off to bed myself,'' she announced. ''We can dissect the party over breakfast tomorrow.''

Janey stretched her arms and flexed her shoulders, stiff from holding Maddy's relaxed weight. Webb, half sitting on the arm of a love seat, was watching her with an odd expression in his eyes. She looked around to see if they were alone, but Albert was silently gathering up used glasses and napkins and canapé plates.

She picked up a couple of abandoned wineglasses and set them on his tray. The butler blanched.

Webb grinned. "You're making Albert nervous again," he observed. "Interfering with his system is something he doesn't take lightly."

"Sorry, Albert," Janey said crisply. "I just thought there was no sense in you staying up any later than necessary to clean up the mess when we could all pitch in and have it done fast."

"Whatever you like, miss," Albert said faintly. He didn't sound convinced.

Webb got up. "Something tells me this calls for mediation. Janey, Albert means he'd rather you just leave him to do his job. And Albert, Ms. Griffin thinks you should put off the rest of the work till morning. So give it a rest for now, both of you. Come on, Janey, I'll walk you upstairs."

In the upper hall, she paused and turned to face him. "What happened? What did he say?"

"Roger Herrington, you mean? Oh, about what you'd expect."

She was nearly as frustrated as Maddy had been with her problem-causing peg. Of course she didn't know what to expect, and Webb obviously understood that—so why couldn't he just give her a straight answer?

On the other hand, she thought, his answer, evasive though it was, made sense. It really wasn't her business, no matter what Webb had told him or how Roger Herrington had reacted—was it? That was strictly between the men who had loved Sibyl.

If this engagement were real, then of course she would have every right to know how the news had been greeted. But as it was…she had no right at all.

She felt a sick emptiness in the pit of her stomach. Had she come so close to losing track of the truth? Had she thrown herself so willingly into playing her part that she'd almost forgotten it was a role and she an actress hired to do the job?

She stopped outside the closed door of her bedroom and looked at the knot of Webb's necktie instead of his face. "I guess I didn't realize how tired I am, Webb. Maybe we can talk about it in the morning, instead."

They wouldn't, of course. But why push him into saying that he had no intention of telling her?

He didn't answer. The tips of his fingers brushed the bare skin at the top of her shoulder and skimmed inward, following the path of a narrow velvet strap, to lightly touch the hollow at the base of her throat. Janey leaned back against the door, trying not to jerk away from him, trying not to let him guess that his simple, gentle touch seemed to reach inside her and take her breath away.

"Every man downstairs wanted to do this tonight." His voice was husky, and his eyes had gone dark.

"None of them tried," Janey replied.

The corner of his mouth quirked upward. "Not till now."

She expected him to pull her close, to repeat the intimate body contact that had made her challenging kiss such an explosive experience. But he didn't. He simply leaned closer, one hand braced against the door frame above her shoulder, his body blocking her from making any move. In effect, he was pinning her against the door without even touching her—until with his index finger he very gently began tracing the edges of each of the velvet straps that held her dress together.

He slowly mapped the outlines of each exposed patch of skin, while she wondered how many there were and how long she could stand the exquisite torture of his exploration. Not only did she feel each brush of his fingertip, but her skin tingled in anticipation of the next touch and in memory of the previous one, until she felt as if she were a violin vibrating under the caress of a virtuoso.

He bent his head and his lips took hers, softly at first, until her treacherous mouth quivered in response and gave him the permission he'd seemed to seek. He kissed her long and deeply, the kiss of a confident lover, nibbling at her lips, teasing and passionate and demanding in turn.

By the time he stopped, Janey's knees were the texture of peanut butter and she was sagging against the door, relying on its support. She tried desperately to pull herself together, to keep him from seeing how overwhelmed she was. "Why did you do that? We're not in public now, so there's nobody to impress. And if you tell me you thought Camilla's door was open just a crack, I won't believe you."

"Then I won't bother to tell you." There was a uneven edge to his voice. "I kissed you because I wanted to. And you kissed me back for the same reason." He leaned a little closer. "I don't suppose you'd like to invite me in?"

Yes, she thought, and was aghast at the ease with which her mind embraced the notion.

"Not on your life," she said.

Webb shrugged. He was so close to her that the gesture felt like her own. "So I'll keep trying."

Janey stumbled across the threshold and leaned once more against the door, this time on the slightly safer side.

It was crazy to want a man who still loved his dead wife, and Janey knew it. She wasn't such a fool as to think that making love and loving were the same thing; what Webb felt for her was politely called desire—or, less politely, lust. She knew he could make love to her once—or a half-dozen times, perhaps—and then walk away, his curiosity satisfied, his desire slaked, without a tinge of regret.

And she knew that if she continued to steadfastly say no, he would continue to accept that—just as casually and cheerfully as he had tonight.

He would enjoy her if she was available, but he wouldn't pace the floor wanting her if she wasn't—because it simply didn't matter all that much to him whether she slept with him or not. Because *she* didn't matter to him.

So why, Janey asked herself miserably, did she feel the almost overwhelming urge to open the door and call him back?

CHAPTER EIGHT

WEBB was already at the breakfast table when Janey came into the gallery on Saturday morning, and Maddy, still in her blue pajamas, was on his lap, half concealed behind his open newspaper. His coffee cup was set off to the side, where Maddy couldn't reach it. Camilla's place had been cleared, except for a used cup, and she was nowhere in sight.

Maddy, her eyes agleam, pushed the newspaper out of her way and scrambled till she was standing on Webb's thigh, holding up her arms to Janey.

Janey hesitated. But it was silly to refuse to pick up Maddy just because she had to come within three feet of Webb to do so. One thing was sure—he wasn't going to grab her for a repetition of that scorching good-night kiss.

And maybe that's why you're so hesitant, Janey told herself rudely. *Because you know he won't—and part of you wishes he would.*

Her hand brushed his sweater sleeve as she picked up the baby. The wool fibers felt like a wire brush against her skin, creating a tingling sensation that was just short of painful. She managed to keep her voice level. "Good morning. I hope you slept well."

Obviously he had; he looked as bright-eyed as Maddy this morning. Being turned down obviously hadn't caused him to fret—but Janey had known better than to think he would lose a minute's rest over her refusal.

And Janey had nothing to feel sensitive about, either, she reminded herself. She'd had an attack of hormones last

131

night, that was all; nothing to feel ashamed of. It happened to every normal woman now and then, sometimes even when there was no logical reason—so it should have come as no surprise to find herself reeling because she'd run up against Webb Copeland in an amorous mood. The man could kiss a marble statue into dust; what mere flesh and blood woman could weather an encounter like that and be unaffected?

The wonder would have been if, after that kiss, she *hadn't* thought about throwing caution to the wind. Her body had proved it was completely normal; the important thing was that her mind had reasserted control in time.

She'd simply be more careful in the future. Last night she'd been too tired to think—and she'd also made the mistake of assuming that without an audience Webb wouldn't bother to put on a show. So, now that she knew better…

Maddy wriggled around in Janey's arms till she was perfectly comfortable.

Webb folded the newspaper and laid it aside. "As a matter of fact, I didn't sleep as well as I could have." If the unspoken message—that he'd have rested much better if she had joined him—hadn't already been plain, the warmth of his gaze drifting over her body would have made it so.

Camilla came in, dressed in a deep pink suit and with every hair perfectly in place. "I think that takes care of all the household consultations for the moment. You'll find, Janey, that with a well-trained staff, running a house this size isn't really complex at all. What plans have you two made for today?"

Webb set his coffee cup down so Albert could refill it. "I thought, if Janey was agreeable, we'd take Maddy down to see the whales and dolphins at Shedd Aquarium."

Almost automatically, Janey said, "I have to study for my test on Monday in my structural performance class."

"Just for the morning," Webb said. "You'll have all afternoon to study and still have time for a nap before dinner."

He didn't wait for a comment, which Janey interpreted to mean he didn't want to hear any further disagreement. And he thought Camilla was bossy sometimes? She wrinkled her nose at him, but she didn't argue; it so obviously would get her nowhere.

Webb said solicitously, "I don't suppose you'd like to go along, Gran?"

"My dear, I wouldn't dream of being a fifth wheel on an adventure like that." Camilla's tone was faintly sarcastic. "However, if you're hoping to run into Roger Herrington there, I don't believe he's on the board of directors anymore."

"I'd forgotten he ever was," Webb said calmly.

Janey bit her tongue. Hadn't he told his grandmother that he'd already talked to Sibyl's father? Curiosity was pinching her like a too-small shoe, and no matter how much she tried to tell herself it was none of her business, it didn't help.

By the time they were in the car, Janey couldn't stand it anymore. "Haven't you told her yet about that call last night?"

"Of course I did—this morning."

"Wasn't she upset that you waited so long?"

"Not when she heard what he'd said."

Janey's voice was very small. "Oh. That bad, hmm?"

"He wasn't very pleased, no."

She cleared her throat. "But that's good news, really—isn't it? I mean, if Sibyl's father went through the roof at the idea of you marrying me, then you'll have to reconsider, and Camilla must think…" She shook her head a little, trying to clear it. "This is all getting far too complicated, you know."

"You couldn't be more right about that. It's way too complex. You're still certain Gran thinks you're impossible—"

"You'd be certain, too, if you'd been in—" She broke off abruptly, unwilling to admit that she'd inspected his bedroom, even if the visit had been at Camilla's instigation. She went on a bit lamely, "If you'd heard what she told me yesterday."

"I've heard her say plenty—and the majority of it contradicts itself. So I think we should simplify the plan."

Janey frowned. "And do what instead?"

"Break my heart."

Warily, Janey looked him over. He didn't appear to have lost all his capacity for reason, but… "Aside from that being impossible, I don't see how you think it'll help."

"I don't mean really break it, of course. But if we were to take this relationship a step farther and have a rip-roaring, passionate, all-consuming affair—"

"I should have known which direction this was going."

"Then, when you break it off—"

"At your direction, of course. And you'll make sure it won't be until you're tired of the whole thing." She was proud of herself for managing to put a tinge of humor in her voice. After all, this incredible suggestion couldn't be anything more than a bad joke—and she wasn't about to take it seriously…

Even if she hadn't quite managed to wipe the memory of last night's shattering kiss from her memory. Even if the longings she thought she'd mastered had surged up again out of nowhere along with the mere suggestion of being his lover. Even if her heart raced and her ears pounded and her body ached to be held close to him.

"If we're going to all the trouble, we may as well enjoy it to the fullest," Webb said pointedly. "Anyway, when it's over, I'll be—to all appearances—nursing a broken heart, which will make Gran leave me alone."

Janey shook her head. "No, she'll just try to catch you on the rebound. And then—" She leaned forward. "That's the most bizarre—"

"I wouldn't call it bizarre," Webb argued. "It seems pretty sensible to me, and at least we'd be able to keep the rules straight for a change."

"Which rules? Oh, I wasn't talking about your crazy idea. I was looking at that house." She waved a hand toward a set of wrought-iron gates they'd just passed. "I've never seen a Gothic-influenced saltbox before."

"That's nothing compared to some of the stuff in this neighborhood."

"Honestly? I've never come this route before—or else it's been too dark to see the details."

"Want me to go around the block so you can get the full effect?"

Janey said frankly, "I'd rather stand on the sidewalk like an ill-bred rustic and stare."

"Well, hanging on to the gates and ogling might not be the most popular of moves. But we can do better than driving round the block—we'll get Maddy's stroller out and use her for cover. If we take the baby for a walk through the neighborhood, you can inspect to your heart's content."

"I could probably gawk all morning," Janey admitted, "and we'd never get to the aquarium. So if it's a big deal to you and Maddy to visit the whales—"

"It's not. But Gran's idea of exciting marine life is the dance floor on a trans-Atlantic liner, so—"

"You chose this expedition deliberately, knowing she wouldn't go along?"

"Confess it, Janey, you're enjoying an hour of not having to watch everything you say."

"Every bit as much as you are." Janey watched in fascination as flecks of gold lighted in his eyes, foreshadowing his smile. He really was a very good-looking man; she could understand why some women would go so nuts over him that they'd think simply having him—even without the possibility of ever securing his love—would be enough.

Webb pulled the car off to the side of the street. As he lifted Maddy's stroller from the trunk and unfolded it, he said casually, "I've never asked what sort of architect you want to be."

"Whatever somebody will offer me a job doing." Janey's voice was crisp. She picked up Maddy from her car seat and settled her in the stroller.

"That's no answer."

"Of course it is. Architects—especially brand-new and untried ones—aren't in such demand that they can be choosy. If I get an offer from an industrial design firm, I'll create factories." She fell into step beside him. "If it's a commercial firm, I'll plan shopping malls. The only thing I'd really hate would be spending my days designing parking ramps. I've never been able to find any humor in the soul of a parking ramp."

"Parking ramps are supposed to have souls?"

"Well, the subject isn't exactly covered in the curriculum—and maybe *personality* would be a better word than *soul*. All good buildings have an extra quality that gives them character. But parking ramps..." She shook her head.

"You didn't say anything at all about designing houses—and yet you seem to love them best."

She shot a look at him. There was a softness in his

voice—a note of understanding—which almost frightened her. "Am I that obvious? I'd love to spend my life creating houses, but—"

"So why not aim for what you want?"

"Because it's the toughest field to break into."

"You don't seem the sort to let competition discourage you."

"That depends entirely on the competition. There are lots of architects—including experienced ones—looking for jobs in home design these days, and there's tremendous rivalry among firms for the relatively few commissions in the field. It's not exactly a growing business."

"It should be. People are building houses all the time."

"Most of them don't hire architects. In fact, most of them don't really care if they have a specially designed house, so they save some money by buying blueprints from a service." She paused in front of the Gothic saltbox's wrought-iron gates.

Webb looked through the bars. "You mean there could be more of *these* scattered across the country?"

Janey smothered a smile at the horror in his voice. "Doubtful. Sometimes people hire a builder who draws up their ideas—or maybe he even combines several commercial designs. I'd bet that's what happened here. There's even a little Tudor influence around the back—see it?"

"If all buildings have souls," Webb began, "then this one—"

"—ought to be locked in the psych ward at Cook County Hospital." She gave the stroller a push. "I might be able to work for a firm that creates stock plans. But..."

Webb would no doubt think her objection to that idea was silly, and Janey had to agree that it was. If she was employed by a stock blueprint firm, she'd be doing the work she liked best—and it was wildly unrealistic to set extra conditions on a job that was almost what she wanted, when she'd said not long ago that she'd do any kind of work just to work in her field.

Webb said, "But you'd like to carry every project all the way through and see the results—and you can't do that sitting in an office drawing houses that may never exist except in your imagination."

Twice now he seemed to have read her mind. And he actually sounded as if he understood. Janey was starting to feel a little shaky at the turns the conversation was taking; this was too private all of a sudden, too revealing. She didn't want him to see so much.

She tried for a twist of humor. "And have so much business that I could turn down any client who doesn't have the right attitude about building," she agreed lightly.

Webb smiled. "You could even make people take a sort of compatibility test, to see if they're worthy of your talent."

"Of course—why didn't I think of that? Unfortunately getting established well enough so I could be at all selective would take years and in the meantime I'm practical enough to want to eat once in a while. To say nothing of all the money I'm going to have to repay. I can't afford to take years to build up a reputation and a practice."

He didn't say anything for a while, and Janey wondered if he was still having trouble believing that she really was planning to pay back every nickel she borrowed.

"You're between a rock and a hard place, aren't you?" he said finally.

Janey frowned. "I don't see what you mean."

"You could keep working so you wouldn't have to borrow so much money, but then you can't devote all your attention to studying, and you can't be sure of graduating high enough in your class to get the kind of job you want.

But if you borrow money so you can spend all your time studying—''

Janey nodded. "I'll have to take any job I'm offered in order to pay it all back. I prefer to think of it as a challenge instead of an impasse." She held her head high. "I've gotten this far, I'll figure out the rest as it comes."

Webb said lightly, "Maybe I'll have you work off the debt."

"By doing what? Designing a new house for you? You'd never give up a Bellows masterpiece—would you?" She looked at him suspiciously.

"That wasn't what I had in mind, no."

"Good." They turned a corner and she spotted a pocket-size park. "I'll race you to the slide."

"Only if you take Maddy as a handicap."

"All right, that leaves you with the stroller." She snatched up the baby and beat Webb by a clear two yards. He didn't even bother climbing the ladder to the top of the slide, just waited at the bottom for the two of them to come down, with Maddy held firmly in Janey's lap.

The baby's eyes were wide, as if she was still debating whether she'd liked the experience. Webb picked her up, and from the safety of his arms she stared long and hard at the slide.

Janey was still sitting at the bottom.

"Will you show me your work?" Webb asked.

She looked up in surprise. "You mean you want to see it?"

"It would be only sensible, wouldn't it? If I like what I see, maybe I'll let you pay off a chunk of your debt by building me a new factory."

"That would be a twist," Janey murmured. "Having the architect work there first to figure out how an assembly line should really be put together."

But how odd it seemed, she thought—even as she said the words—that she hardly remembered working for him, moving steel on the factory floor, running the machines. In just these few days away from her job, the memory of it had faded till it was the same thin texture as the recollection of her high school prom.

Or perhaps it wasn't so strange. She'd been snatched up from the scullery and swept off to the ball—no wonder she didn't want to remember the ashes and the scrubbing! But she'd better not forget that this Cinderella life-style was only going to last for another twenty-four hours.

She watched Webb as he tickled Maddy, sending her into waves of helpless baby giggles. As he played with his daughter, Webb looked as happy as she'd ever seen him. That was exactly as it should be, Janey told herself firmly. He'd gone into this masquerade for Maddy's sake, and he knew that in another week or two, the purpose would be accomplished. He would be free of encumbrances—free to simply love his daughter.

Janey was pleased for him.

Truly, she was.

They wandered the neighborhood all morning to look at houses and stopped at the edge of the nearest commercial district to eat hamburgers in a storefront restaurant. By the time they'd finished, a few enormous snowflakes had started to drift from the sky, and Maddy leaned out of the stroller till she almost tipped it over, trying to catch them.

Only then did Webb realize that he couldn't quite remember where he'd left the car, and they spent almost an hour trying to retrace their steps. By the time they'd found the right street, Janey—with her hazel eyes alight and a dusting of snowflakes sparkling in her honey brown hair—was teasing that if he was no more attached to his Jaguar than to lose it less than six blocks from home, he might as well give it to her and start taking the bus himself.

He retaliated, to Maddy's delight, by collecting a few enormous flakes and putting them down the back of Janey's neck. He didn't know what she might have done in return, for just then they turned a corner and spotted the car.

The morning's fresh air and exercise took its toll. Webb's intention, after Janey went off to study, was simply to rock Maddy to sleep, but he sent himself into oblivion as well.

When he roused, with Maddy still soundly sleeping in his arms, the library was dim except for the flicker of flames from a newly rebuilt fire. From his deep leather chair, he could see the parlor, where his grandmother occupied her usual low rocker with her knitting—pale yellow this time—in her lap. Sitting cross-legged on the hearth rug nearby was Janey.

She seemed to sense that he was awake, though Webb didn't think he'd even moved, and in one swift and graceful motion she came to her feet.

She'd said she hadn't been a dancer. Nevertheless, she moved like one. How had he ever mistaken that loose-limbed, easy walk of hers—even encumbered as it had been by those heavy, awkward, steel-toed shoes—for a lack of grace?

Janey paused just inside the library, leaning against the door casing. "I came down a while ago to see if you needed a hand with Maddy, but obviously you have everything under control."

Just behind her, the butler cleared his throat. "Excuse me, sir," he said. "Mrs. Wilson wanted me to tell you she's back and ready to take over."

Webb's eyes narrowed and his gaze went automatically to Camilla, who still rocked placidly with needles flashing, never missing a beat. She'd been quite confident at first that the woman would be back by Saturday, he thought, and the suspicion grew that she'd arranged this little interlude in order to test how well Janey and Maddy would get along together.

Still, he had to admit, when Mrs. Wilson appeared in the doorway a moment later, that she wasn't exactly the picture of vitality; in fact, her face was almost as white as her uniform.

Her eyes, however, were as sharp as ever, and when she saw the baby sprawled across his lap asleep, her jaw tightened. "I'll take Madeline upstairs now, sir."

"She's fine where she is," Webb said levelly. "I'll bring her up when she wakes."

"Letting her sleep on your lap like that is simply asking for trouble," the nurse snapped. "No doubt she's been so thoroughly spoiled in the last couple of days that it'll take weeks to overcome it all."

Janey, who had been standing absolutely still next to the doorway, moved forward into the nurse's line of sight. "Perhaps," she said, "it shouldn't be overcome at all. Just maybe Maddy could stand a little spoiling—since you seem to think giving her ordinary attention is spoiling her." She held Mrs. Wilson's gaze for a long moment and then walked out of the library.

Webb didn't even watch her go. He was too busy enjoying the shock on Mrs. Wilson's face. If Maddy had suddenly started singing grand opera, the nurse couldn't have looked more astounded.

The restaurant Webb had chosen was one Janey had never heard of, which of course didn't surprise her. Chicago must have a thousand restaurants that she would probably never set foot inside.

But this one was obviously the most exclusive of the exclusive. Located in a converted brownstone town house, it strove to maintain the look and atmosphere of a private home, with only a few wide-spaced tables in each of the dining rooms.

The maître d' led them to the farthest room, where there were just four tables—all of them empty. Webb held her chair.

"Private dining room?" Janey asked. "I'm not sure if I should be impressed with you for your obvious status or offended at the maître d' for wanting to keep me away from his other patrons."

"Neither," Webb said. "There are reservation cards on all the other tables."

Janey shrugged Camilla's mink jacket from her shoulders to drape over the back of her chair. The gesture might look nonchalant; at least she hoped it did. But her fingertips caressed the soft, slick fur. She hadn't exactly wanted to borrow the jacket, but Camilla had insisted, and Janey would have been lying if she'd said she regretted the order. What an incredible feeling it was, to treat almost casually something of such incredible beauty. She'd never experienced anything quite so luxurious, and she would never have the chance again.

You're Cinderella, she reminded herself. *And midnight's approaching.*

Webb finished conferring with the waiter and the wine steward, and as soon as they were gone Janey leaned forward, determined to clear her conscience. "I'm sorry about interfering this afternoon when Mrs. Wilson came back. It's none of my business, and I'll be more careful."

"Don't worry about it. I enjoyed watching her face while you told her I wasn't spoiling Maddy."

Janey told herself to stop while she was ahead. She'd

made her apology, and he'd been more gracious about it than she'd expected. Even if the engagement had been real, her involvement with Maddy's care wouldn't extend to hiring and firing the help. After the wedding, of course, it would be different. But since there wasn't going to be a wedding…

But her tongue wouldn't be stilled. "Actually, Webb, if you let Maddy get in the habit of sleeping in your arms, you'll end up with a little girl who won't want to use her bed at all. You'll be frustrated and she'll be horrid."

Two small lines cut ridges between his brows. "Then why did you speak up? If you agree with Mrs. Wilson—"

"I never said I questioned her competence," she said unhappily. "It's just that the woman's almighty attitude makes me sizzle."

"You're *certain* you're not studying how to impress Gran? She and Mrs. Wilson have been fighting a cold war since the day Gran moved in—so taking her side would certainly win you points."

That was odd, Janey thought, for he seemed to mean that Mrs. Wilson had seniority, of a sort—that she'd already been in the house when Camilla came. But of course Camilla couldn't have actually moved immediately after Sibyl died; she'd have had a house, or an apartment maybe, to deal with. And Maddy hadn't even been two months old, he'd said. Of course he'd hired a nurse right away.

He'd sounded almost amused, she realized. That must mean he'd finally given up the notion that she was trying to maneuver him into making this pretense true. As if she could.

Or would want to, she thought. There was nothing less likely than that, and it was about time Webb recognized it.

The wine steward reappeared with a dusty bottle, which he expertly uncorked. Webb tasted the wine and nodded, and the wine steward filled their glasses and silently went away once more.

Janey stared into the depths of the dark ruby liquid. "Do the Herringtons see a lot of Maddy?"

Webb had raised his glass to take a sip, and he didn't answer right away. "Not much. I think they'll be more interested when she's older."

Janey didn't understand how anyone could look at Maddy and not be ready to sign papers as an indentured servant just for the pleasure of watching her grow. But she also knew, from seeing Sibyl's portrait, just how much Maddy looked like her mother. The child must be a reminder to the Herringtons, even more than she was to Webb, of what they had lost. Perhaps, instead of a comfort, that was torture to parents who had lost a child.

The explanation wasn't bad, but it still couldn't satisfy her. To choose not to be involved with Maddy…she didn't get it.

The waiter had brought their appetizers. She frowned at the little heap of lavishly decorated trout mousse.

Webb had picked up his fork, but he set it aside. "Is there something wrong with the mousse?"

Curious as she was, Janey could hardly ask him for an explanation of the Herringtons' behavior. She'd already intruded far enough into things that weren't her business, but to interrogate him about the inner motives of his in-laws would definitely be crossing the line.

She poked the mousse. "Of course not. I was just thinking—I know it's silly, this place is lovely. But I sort of liked lunch better. Maddy trying to take a bite out of your hamburger…" The mere memory made her smile. "She could handle the mousse much better."

"So next time we should bring her? It'd be worth it just to see the maître d's face."

But of course, Janey reminded herself, there wouldn't be a next time, and she took a deep breath and resolved to enjoy this evening twice as much.

Over their steaks, she asked, tentatively, "Are you really going to build a new factory?"

"Probably. Without it, even with the third shift at full strength, we'll be running continually behind. Why?"

She cut a tiny bite from her filet mignon, watching her knife as if she was conducting a surgical maneuver of the utmost importance. "You said before... Would you really consider..." Her voice trailed off.

"Giving you the job?"

She shook her head. "Oh, no. I wouldn't expect you to limit yourself like that. But if you'd let me have a chance at it, Webb...if I could just submit my ideas along with the others who'll want the commission..." She looked up, finally.

He was staring at her, utter astonishment turning his eyes deep brown, and he shook his head just a little.

Janey's heart dropped like a lump of lead. She took a deep breath and tried to smile. "Of course I knew you were joking."

"I hardly recognize you," Webb said. "This is the same Janey who just a few days ago held me up for an indecent amount of money?"

"You know perfectly well why I need that money, and that I plan to pay it back."

"That's why I can't believe you're being tentative now. You'll have to develop some confidence, you know, if this is going to be your profession."

"You mean you weren't saying no?"

"Of course not. I'm in business. I'm not going to limit myself to one set of blueprints when I can get an extra free."

Janey tilted her chin up. "I never said I'd do the whole design for free—just the preliminaries."

Webb grinned. "That's more like it. Someday you'll be able to look somebody in the eye and quote an absolutely outrageous price...and get it."

"And I can practice on you," Janey agreed sweetly.

They lingered over coffee and bananas Foster, and it was late when the waiter brought the bill. Janey wanted to pretend that the evening would never end and drag it out by any means possible. But she had more dignity than that, so she smiled at him and said, "It's been lovely, Webb."

He signed the ticket and handed the leather folder back to the waiter. "Better thank Gran," he said lightly.

Janey's stomach twisted into a knot at the reminder that the evening had in no way been his idea. But she had too much pride to let him see, so she fussed over Camilla's fur jacket instead.

The outer dining rooms were as full as when they'd come in, with a few late arrivals waiting in the lobby for the maître d's attention. Janey would bet that one of the women could value Camilla's jacket down to the penny, her inspection was so close. Then her gaze slid from Janey to Webb, and her eyebrows lifted almost expectantly, Janey thought.

"What a coincidence to see you here," Webb said, with a tinge of irony. "Marilyn, I'd like you to meet—"

"No, you wouldn't," the woman said. Her voice was low; despite the cultured tones, there was a harsh note in it that seemed to scrape Janey's nerves raw. "So this is what you're going to put in my Sibyl's place."

Webb took his overcoat from the rack next to the front door. "Not *what*," he said coolly. *"Who."* He draped the coat over his arm and put a firm hand on Janey's elbow.

She had frozen to the spot, staring at the woman who

could only be Sibyl's mother. Now that she knew, she could see the woman's resemblance to Sibyl's portrait. It lay more in the shape of the face than in the coloration; Marilyn Herrington's hair was dark blond and her eyes blue.

"Jack Baxter told us you'd introduced him to your fiancée," Marilyn said.

"So that's it. I didn't think Roger was surprised. I should have expected Jack would come running to make sure you knew. And of course that explains how you happened to be dining here tonight, too."

"I had to see for myself. We could hardly believe what Jack said. We thought surely he'd misunderstood, so when he said you were coming here tonight..." Her gaze flicked over Janey once more. "And what a choice you've made. He said she had no more taste than to go into Coq Au Vin wearing jeans."

Webb's eyes were cool, but the corner of his mouth quirked. "Did he also tell you how she looks in jeans? Almost—but not quite—better than she looks in that dress."

"It certainly couldn't be worse than she looks in Camilla's fur," Marilyn Herrington said crisply. "Like a little girl playing dress-up before she has the faintest notion how to conduct herself."

The insult was so biting that Janey's breath caught in her throat. Half-consciously she raised her hand, as if she could clear the blockage, and Marilyn Herrington's gaze seemed to burn through Janey's fingers.

"Is that Sibyl's ring?" She leaned forward, her face suddenly as sharp as an eagle's.

"It certainly isn't," Webb said.

There was a note of relief in the woman's voice. "At least you've maintained that much good taste. I can't say much for the rest, but thank heaven you still have some sense of what you owe our girl.'' A tall white-haired man came in from the street and Marilyn Herrington beckoned him to her side. ''Roger, don't you think that under the circumstances we should keep Sibyl's ring, so it'll be safe for Madeline one day? As things are—''

''I think,'' Webb said crisply, ''that perhaps you should mind your own business.''

Roger Herrington said, ''Young man, I will not allow you—''

''And as for what I owe your girl,'' Webb said, ''you force me to remind you that her life is over, and I don't owe her—or you—the rest of mine. If you cannot be polite to my fiancée, then I expect you to keep your distance.''

Every separate cell of Janey's body was trembling in its own independent rhythm. But it wasn't the attack that had caused her shakiness, she realized in astonishment. Though actually meeting the Herringtons had taken her off guard, their reaction hadn't been much of a surprise.

No, she was quivering because he had defended her. Webb had stood up for her.

How sweet it would be if he had meant it.

That was when she knew, in a brilliant and horrifying flash of insight, that all her efforts to keep her distance from him, to maintain her balance and her sense of humor so she could walk away with a smile when this was over, had been in vain.

Like Cinderella he had swept her out of the scullery and into the castle, and—like Cinderella—she had fallen in love with Prince Charming.

And there was nothing she could do now to turn back the clock.

CHAPTER NINE

THE revelation that had hit Janey wasn't so much like a brilliant spotlight throwing her problem into clear view as it was a strobe that with each almost-blinding flash revealed another snatch of understanding. The same was true of her physical surroundings; suddenly instead of normal movement she seemed to be seeing stop-action photos—the fury in Marilyn Herrington's face, the wrath on her husband's, the shock in the eyes of the onlookers.

Webb didn't take her elbow to guide her out; he put his arm around her shoulders instead. The cold wind that whistled down the street and whipped the awning above the restaurant's entrance made her shiver despite the weight of Camilla's fur jacket. Janey wanted nothing more than to bury her face in Webb's broad shoulder—but that, she was afraid, had little to do with the wind.

He tossed his keys to the valet and looked down at Janey. "Sorry about making you wait in the cold. After that little scene—"

She didn't look at him. "They're obviously still in terrible pain."

Just as you are, she wanted to add. *Only you're feeling guilty, to boot.* By bringing Janey into the mixture—pretending to be serious about her, forcing comparisons between her and Sibyl—he'd rubbed salt in the Herringtons' wounds. Perhaps he'd only just now realized the full extent of their hurt, and that was why he'd been so prickly and made things even worse.

"I think you should tell them the truth," she said quietly.

For a moment she thought he wasn't going to answer. "They'll know soon enough."

"It's worse for them. Your grandmother doesn't approve, either, but I'm not like torture to her. To the Herringtons—"

"It isn't you, Janey. They'd object to anyone."

"But that's the whole point, Webb. You owe them the truth. Tell them that there isn't anyone at all."

And don't you forget the lesson, either, she told herself. *There is no one who can take Sibyl's place in his life and his heart. Certainly not you.*

Janey was subdued on the drive home, though she knew she was no more quiet than Webb was. She almost felt grateful to Marilyn Herrington for giving them the excuse to be silent. Her mind was churning, still stunned by what she had learned about herself tonight.

She'd never believed in love at first sight. Of course, she'd never given the subject much thought; when there weren't enough hours in the day to fit in work, study and sleep, who had time to fret about finding love? But she'd always assumed that love took its time, that it developed slowly and silently, almost secretly...

Well, that much was consistent, she thought dryly. She'd had no warning; this had crept up on her like a silent stalker.

She tried to tell herself that it was too soon for love, that what she was feeling was infatuation instead. She couldn't have fallen in love in a matter of days. She didn't love him, she *wouldn't* love him, because it was too impractical, too hurtful, too difficult.

And also too terribly real. She could try till Lake Michigan froze over to convince herself, and it wasn't going to make any difference—because deep in her heart she knew the truth.

She'd been startled when she'd realized that her memories of work had faded. Now she knew that hadn't happened because she disliked the job so much that a few days away from it let her blank out her mind, but because she'd spent those days with Webb. And it wasn't because of the perks—the house, the staff, the dresses, the dinners out— that she had treasured those days. It wouldn't have mattered if they'd camped out in a cave, for it was Webb who had created the magic. Laughing with him, talking with him, sharing with him...loving him.

Webb's touch, as he helped her out of the car, was almost impersonal, and though he walked Janey to her room he didn't even take her hand. It was almost as if he was afraid that throwing his arm around her in that dramatic gesture at the restaurant might lead her to expect more. And though last night he'd been quite obviously willing to explore the limits, tonight was a different story. Seeing the Herringtons, being reminded of Sibyl, having to admit the hurt his scam was causing...it didn't matter why, Janey told herself, but the change in him was all too apparent.

She put a hand on the doorknob and deliberately didn't turn to face him, for he might interpret that as an invitation to kiss her, and she didn't want to take the chance of seeing reluctance or regret in his eyes. She'd remember last night instead, when he had teased her...desired her.

"Janey," he said, and his fingertips brushed her nape. "You're an awfully good sport, you know."

She nodded and slipped through the door into her darkened bedroom. So that was what he thought of her, was it? *An awfully good sport.*

That careless accolade was light years from what she wanted from him. But it was all she could have—and she must not allow herself to forget it.

*   *   *

Instead of going into his own room, Webb found himself at the closed door of the big master bedroom, hand on the knob. He hesitated, almost as if the room were a safe and he couldn't quite recall the combination needed to open it, while conflicting emotions warred within him. Eventually, very slowly, he pushed the door open and stepped into the room he hadn't faced in more than a year.

There was no hint of staleness or dust; the staff obviously took care of this abandoned room just as faithfully as Albert laid out the unused silk pajamas on Webb's pillow every night. But it was just as obviously empty; the scent of Sibyl's perfume was gone. Even the lacy peignoir, which lay across the chaise longue no longer smelled of Midnight Passion.

He walked across the deep plush carpet to stand by the fireplace, under the portrait of Sibyl. He rested an elbow on the mantel and looked up at her. A chance shaft of moonlight came through the front windows and caressed the lovely face.

Beautiful, charming Sibyl—so senselessly dead.

Tell them the truth, Janey had urged. And he would, he concluded. He'd tell the Herringtons the truth.

Just as soon as he figured out what it was.

After dinner on Sunday Janey curled up in one of the big leather chairs in the library to finish studying for her test the next day, but she found it hard to concentrate. Not only was her mind prone to sliding away from structural performance statistics and onto the hopelessness of loving a man who was still devoted to a dead wife, but a restless Webb seemed to be pacing the entire house.

The third time he came into the library, Janey put her book aside and said, ''Whatever it is that you've been working up your nerve to say, I wish you'd just spit it out.

If you're hesitating to tell me that you're ready to take me home, you don't have to tiptoe around the idea. The weekend's almost over anyway, so what do a few hours one way or the other matter?''

"You want to go home?"

"There I could study in peace," Janey said pointedly.

"Sorry. I didn't mean to annoy you. I guess it's just that with Maddy back in the nursery, the whole house seems pretty dead."

"All fifteen thousand square feet of it," she said dryly, and began to gather up her books. "I'll run upstairs and finish the last of my packing, and then all I need to do is say goodbye to Camilla."

She didn't wait for an answer, but she was afraid that she saw a tinge of relief in his face. Had he been worried that she might make a fuss about leaving? *It would serve him right,* Janey thought irritably, *if I fell down the stairs and broke my leg and had to stay till the cast came off!*

She'd put most of her things in the bag as she dressed that morning, feeling with every garment and toiletry that her heart was breaking. It took only a couple of minutes to gather the rest and make sure that she'd left the dresses Camilla had bought her hanging neatly in the closet.

She took one last look around the room in an effort to imprint every detail in her mind, though she didn't expect she'd have any trouble remembering it all. Then she picked up her overnight bag and her backpack.

With her first step into the hallway she changed her mind. Webb wouldn't be expecting her to come down for a few minutes, at least, and—despite all her good intentions—she couldn't stand to leave without seeing Maddy one last time. If she didn't make a fuss, didn't announce that it *was* the last time…surely it wouldn't upset the baby as long as she didn't do something foolish like burst into tears. And it would do a little to soothe Janey's own aching heart.

She set her bags back into her room and walked quietly down the hall to the nursery suite. One last hug from Maddy—yes, it was worth braving Mrs. Wilson to get that.

Precious Maddy—the darling of her father's heart, the image of her mother, the innocent reason for this whole masquerade. A hug from Maddy, Janey thought, would be worth almost anything.

She didn't bother to knock but just pushed the nursery door open, as she'd gotten in the habit of doing over the last few days in imitation of Webb and Camilla. Only when she heard Mrs. Wilson's voice did Janey realize that the nurse might be offended at the breach of her privacy. After all, the nursery was not only Mrs. Wilson's workplace, but her bedroom opened directly off it.

Janey was relieved to see that at least the nurse didn't have a guest actually in the room; she was holding the telephone instead. Her back was to Janey, and her voice was soft. "I'm on my way out right now. Be ready."

Janey tapped on the open door, and the woman wheeled around. The look that crossed her face was only slightly short of hatred, Janey thought with a chill.

"I should have expected that *you* wouldn't consider personal privacy to be a concern," Mrs. Wilson snapped.

"Excuse me," Janey said coolly. "I didn't think."

A snowsuited bundle that was nearly as round as it was tall toddled toward her. "Ma!"

Janey picked up the baby. "I just came to say goodbye to Maddy."

The nurse's voice was chilly. "It's not a convenient time. I have Madeline ready to go out for a walk just now." She reached for the child.

Janey counted to ten. "I can see that. Surely it can wait

a minute or two.'' She turned her back on the nurse and tried to cuddle Maddy. She could hardly feel the child's wiry little body inside the bulky snowsuit, and Maddy's face was almost lost behind a scarf tied around her head.

Mrs. Wilson was tapping her foot. ''She'll get over-heated and end up with a cold.''

Janey ignored her. She tried to fight back her tears so she could concentrate on the important things—Maddy's delightful clean-baby smell, the huge brown eyes, the soft-as-velvet cheek—so she could remember them always. She hadn't intended to get attached to this precious baby. Staying aloof had been a sensible plan, but an impossible one, and now she'd give her life for this child.

She drew in one last long breath of Maddy's scent and handed her to Mrs. Wilson. Half blinded by tears, she turned to leave the nursery and tripped over a bulky diaper bag, which was sitting by the door.

She stooped to set it upright and left without bothering to say goodbye to Mrs. Wilson.

She was at the bottom of the stairs, her overnight bag in one hand, her backpack slung over her shoulder, when the nagging doubt at the back corner of her mind exploded into full-fledged suspicion.

That had been a very full diaper bag—amazingly heavy to take along on a walk, especially since Mrs. Wilson wasn't likely to be changing Maddy's diaper on a park bench on a twenty-degree day in November. And why were they going out on a day like this, anyway? In her snowsuit, Maddy would stay toasty warm—but why would Mrs. Wilson, presumably just recovering from a bout of flu, want to go for a walk on such a cold and gloomy day?

And the look she had given Janey…it hadn't been en-tirely hatred. There had been surprise mixed in. And fear. And *guilt*.

She dropped her overnight case and almost flung her backpack; the heavy bag thumped against the marble floor and brought Albert from the back hall with a rare look of surprise on his face. "Are you all right, Miss?"

"Where's Webb?" Janey demanded.

"In the television room, I believe. Can I—"

That figured—he was as far away as he could possibly be and stay within the confines of the house.

Janey glanced up the stairs, but the nurse was not in sight. "Slow Mrs. Wilson down, will you?" She didn't wait for an answer but hurried across the hall, skidded around the corner and ran flat out toward the room where she'd studied on Thanksgiving afternoon, the room where Maddy had fallen asleep in her arms.

Webb stood up as she came in. "I know you said you were ready, but I didn't realize you were so eager to get home."

At the note of humor in his voice, Janey pulled herself up short. Was she just being ridiculous? What did she really have to be suspicious of, anyway? A well-prepared nurse taking a baby for a stroll... He'd probably think she was being silly, or worse.

But she couldn't take the chance. "Mrs. Wilson's taking Maddy for a walk." She was breathless, and the words hurt as she gasped them out.

Webb lifted an eyebrow. "And? Am I supposed to applaud or commiserate?"

"Just...just come and see her."

"Who? Maddy?"

"Mrs. Wilson. There's something wrong, Webb...she was on the phone when I went into the nursery, planning to meet someone." She knew she wasn't making sense— why shouldn't the nurse meet a friend and share a walk?—

so instead she seized his arm and tried to physically pull him toward the door. "Please…"

He frowned, but something in her face seemed to convince him, and he strode toward the front door with Janey close behind.

In the hallway, Maddy had flopped full-length on the marble floor while Albert fussed with the half-unfolded stroller. He seemed to be having trouble getting the latches fixed in place, and Mrs. Wilson was watching in annoyance. "Here, let me do it," she said.

Albert looked relieved when he saw Webb and Janey come around the corner, and he handed over the job without hesitation. "I was only trying to help, Mrs. Wilson," he stated.

"With that kind of help I'd never get out of here," she muttered. She snapped the stroller together with little more than a flick of her wrist and was squatting down beside Maddy to pick her up when she saw Webb and Janey.

The way her gaze flickered between them was enough confirmation for Janey. Then the nurse smiled with what looked like determination. "Say goodbye to your daddy, Madeline."

"Going for a walk?" Webb asked genially. "I think we'll go along. We sort of got in the habit in the last few days, and I could use the exercise. Janey?"

"Um…sure." She slipped past Albert and snatched a couple of coats at random from the guest closet.

"I don't…" Mrs. Wilson began.

But there was no excuse she could give, Janey thought. She could hardly say that having Maddy's father walking beside the stroller would be a detriment to the child.

"Perhaps it's a bit cold after all," the nurse said.

"Oh, no." Webb's voice was expansive. "We might

only go around the block, but the fresh air will be good for all of us. Can I help you with the stroller?''

Mrs. Wilson's mouth set into a hard line. ''No, thank you.'' She maneuvered the stroller across the threshold.

''Shouldn't you just stop her?'' Janey hissed.

''And accuse her of what?'' Webb stuck one arm into the coat Janey handed him and paused. ''I think I'd look a little odd in Gran's fur jacket, don't you?''

''Oh, sorry. Just don't lose sight of that stroller.''

''Don't worry.'' He tossed the fur to Albert, grabbed a parka from Janey's hands and was still putting it on when he reached the front steps.

Janey, a mere half step behind him, bumped hard into his back when he stopped short on the threshold. ''What?''

She leaned around him and saw, as he obviously had, a luxurious black car pulling up in front of the house.

''That's Roger Herrington's Cadillac,'' Webb said.

Janey groaned. ''Great timing for a drop-in visit.''

''Yes, isn't it?'' He leaped the front steps with a bound.

A peculiar note in his voice clicked inside Janey's brain. *Of course,* she thought. *She's got half of Maddy's wardrobe in that diaper bag because she's going to hand her over to them.*

Last night Marilyn Herrington had practically demanded Sibyl's ring in order to keep it safe from Janey. Now the Herringtons had apparently decided they wanted to keep Maddy safe as well—but instead of demanding, they were prepared to simply take her.

Webb reached the Cadillac only a half second behind Mrs. Wilson, with Janey close behind. He leaned against the car door and said, ''Stopping to have a chat, Mrs. Wilson?''

She drew herself upright. ''And why not? They're the child's grandparents.''

"I wasn't aware you were so well acquainted." He tapped on the window, and slowly it descended. Marilyn Herrington glared at him.

"How nice of you to stop by," Webb said.

The car's engine roared for a moment as if it might speed off with Webb still leaning on the door, and then settled back to a whisper and finally to silence as Roger Herrington turned off the ignition. "We came to have a talk with you, my boy."

"Really?" Webb said grimly. "Then of course you must come in. Come back in with us, Mrs. Wilson. We can all have our walk later. I'm sure Maddy's grandparents would be disappointed to miss her."

Janey watched Marilyn Herrington's mouth twist into a very unattractive shape.

Janey had put one hand on the stroller the moment she was within reach, and she kept it there even as Mrs. Wilson meekly pushed Maddy back to the house. She preempted the nurse to take the baby out of the stroller herself, and carried Maddy to the farthest corner of the parlor before she started to unfasten the snowsuit. If anybody was still planning to snatch the child and run, Janey thought, they'd at least have farther to go.

Camilla was in the parlor, sitting in her low rocker with the ever-growing mass of yellow yarn in her lap. "What a surprise," she murmured. "Surely I needn't say it's a pleasant one?" The words were unexceptionable, but Janey had heard that faintly malicious note in her voice before. It was rather pleasant to hear it directed at someone other than herself.

"Albert," Camilla murmured, "bring tea, please—something tells me cocktails would not be a good idea. And perhaps the cook has some goodies on hand to nibble?"

The Herringtons sat down side by side on a couch, Mrs.

Wilson perched on the edge of a straight chair beside the door and Webb—still wearing the parka—planted himself on the arm of a wingchair, his feet braced.

Janey finally managed to release the last fastener and lifted Maddy out of her snowsuit. The baby looked around, goggled wide-eyed at her grandparents and hid her face against Janey's shoulder.

Despite the grim silence in the room, Camilla—the consummate hostess—carried on. "To what do we owe this honor?" she asked the Herringtons.

It was Webb who answered. "To an unrestrained urge to commit a kidnapping, I think."

Camilla clicked her tongue. "My dear, if you wouldn't *mind* taking off your coat…"

"It's not kidnapping to protect a child from harm," Marilyn Herrington burst out.

Webb's voice was cold. "That's a matter of definition. What you call harm is certainly not what I believe it is."

"That's the point," Marilyn said stubbornly. "You're planning to destroy our granddaughter's environment, expose her to an uncultured and ignorant—"

"That's enough." Webb's voice could have cut glass.

Marilyn drew back in shock, but she wasn't quite finished yet. "Look at her," she said, and gestured at Maddy, still hiding her face against Janey's breast.

"I am," Webb said. "And Maddy looks quite contented—apart from being a bit frightened by what's going on. Would you like Janey to hand her over and see if she's as thrilled to sit on your knee?"

"We're not going to stand by while you ruin this child, Webb." Roger Herrington's voice was deep and calm.

"You've certainly been willing to stand by until now," Webb said.

"We've already talked to our attorney." Roger reached for his wife's hand.

Webb's eyebrows raised. "And he approved of this little stunt?"

Roger didn't answer. "He's going to file the papers tomorrow so we'll get custody."

"Sure of that, are you?" Webb said softly. "Then why try to snatch her today?"

"We didn't dare take the chance of you being warned," Marilyn said sullenly. "Maybe spiriting her away."

Webb stood up. "That's it. Get out."

"No." Janey's throat was raw with pain. "This has gotten entirely out of hand."

Albert came in with a huge silver tray. "Thank you," Camilla said tranquilly. "Would you like a cup of tea, Marilyn? Roger?"

Marilyn ignored her. Roger shook his head.

"Webb," Janey said, "they're acting out of love and concern for Maddy. Can't you see that?"

Webb shook his head. "A misguided kind of love."

"Of course it is. They're doing it because they don't want Maddy under my influence. But you told me you thought they wouldn't be any happier if it was someone other than me—didn't you?"

"I suppose I did." Webb sounded grudging.

"And I think you're right." She turned to face Marilyn and Roger. "You're still in such pain over losing your daughter that you'd resent anybody Webb married. And you'd resent Webb for putting her in Sibyl's place."

"Janey," Webb warned. "Don't you dare—"

She raised her voice. "But that's the point. He doesn't want to put anyone in Sibyl's place. This whole confrontation is stupid and pointless and unnecessary."

"Stop it, Janey." Webb's voice was like the crack of a whip.

"*No*. It's past time, Webb." Janey looked straight at Camilla. "There is no engagement. There never has been. Just an agreement to pretend for a while."

Roger and Marilyn gaped at her. Webb swore under his breath. Camilla smiled like a cat who had just spotted a saucer of cream and said, "Would you like both milk and sugar in your tea, Janey?"

Janey shook her head in astonishment. "Nothing, thanks."

Marilyn's voice quavered. "But… But Jack told us… And Webb said last night…and you're wearing a diamond…"

Janey's voice softened. "Webb wanted Camilla to stop pressuring him to get married again. He thought if he brought home someone completely unsuitable…" She had to stop for a moment, because it hurt so much to breathe. "Someone like me…that she'd be so horrified—and so relieved when he dumped me—that she'd leave him alone."

Camilla held up a teacup and sent an inquiring look in Webb's direction. His scowl was apparently answer enough, for she filled the cup and settled back to drink it herself.

"But he didn't stop to think about how it would affect everyone else," Janey went on. "The truth is he never intended to marry me. Or anybody else."

The very silence seemed to echo, until Camilla said placidly, "By the way, Janey…you might want to check the front of your blouse before you stand up. Maddy seems to have taught herself to undo buttons."

Janey looked down at Maddy's delighted face and the gaping front of her blouse, which showed off more than a hint of pink lace on the bra underneath, and choked on a half-hysterical laugh. What a perfect finishing touch to a perfectly horrid afternoon!

Maddy giggled and clapped her hands, and when Janey began to refasten her buttons the baby wrinkled her nose and started to work once more. Janey won the race by handing Maddy to Webb, but the baby leaned out of his arms and reached for Janey. "Ma!" she said desperately.

Janey ruffled her hair. "You only love me for my buttons, Maddy," she said, and smiled even though it hurt. She looked up at Webb for a split second, long enough to see exasperation in his eyes, and tugged the diamond ring from her left hand. She held it out to him, but Maddy's little fist reached out, too, and knocked it from Janey's grip. The ring spun across the room, bounced on the Oriental rug and came to rest next to Camilla's rocker.

"I'll be going now." Janey was eager to say it herself before he could tell her to leave.

His voice was low and level. "You had your say, but you needn't think you can just walk out on me before I have mine."

Maddy, robbed of both Janey and the sparkling gemstone, shrieked at the top of her lungs.

"Talking it over is a lovely sentiment, but this is hardly the place or the time, Webb," Camilla said firmly.

She can't wait to be rid of me. "Later, all right?" Janey said. "It looks to me as if you have your hands full right now, Webb, and you know where to find me."

She left the room in utter silence, realizing almost absently as she passed that Mrs. Wilson's chair was empty. Somewhere in the midst of the mess, the nurse had exercised her self-protective instincts and slipped out. Janey wasn't surprised. She'd have ducked that scene herself if she could.

Her bags were no longer where she had flung them in

her haste to reach Webb, and she had to seek out the ever-efficient Albert to get them back. He interrupted the errand, however, to help Marilyn Herrington into her coat, and Janey waited with all the patience she could muster.

Roger Herrington cleared his throat and said, almost diffidently, "Miss...Griffin, isn't it? Could we offer you a ride somewhere?"

Janey tried to smile. "That's very sweet. But I think I'll walk. I have a lot of things to think about."

He nodded, and a moment later they were gone. Albert retrieved Janey's bags from a hidden cupboard at the back of the hall—one which didn't appear on the floor plans she'd seen. She was momentarily distracted, wondering how many other little secrets Henry Bellows had built into this masterpiece—and then reminded herself that she would never know, because she would never set foot inside this house again.

Albert helped her into her serviceable old coat as respectfully as if it had been Camilla's mink, and she picked up her bags once more.

From the parlor came the gentle creak of Camilla's rocker. "Here's the ring, Webb. You won't want to lose track of that."

Janey heard the deep note of Webb's voice, but she couldn't make out the words.

Camilla said, sounding very calm, "You got caught, didn't you, my dear? Playing games like that—"

I'm ashamed of you. She didn't have to say it, Janey thought. It was there in the tone of her voice, and if Janey could hear it, then Webb—with a whole lot more years of experience—couldn't possibly miss it.

"Miss Griffin?" Albert said hesitantly. "I just wanted to say I'm sorry. Everybody on the staff will be."

It was very nearly the last straw, but with the dregs of

her pride Janey managed to grit her teeth and swallow her
tears and nod her thanks for his concern.

As the front door closed behind her, she half turned to
look up for one last time at the Bellows mansion, which
had held the most pleasant moments of her life.

She had thought that morning as she packed her bags
that her heart was breaking simply because the magical
weekend was over. Now she knew that pain had been a
mere pinprick. This one was like having every nerve in her
body ripped loose, one at a time.

She didn't feel like Cinderella anymore—not even the
version in the scullery. She felt like the pumpkin, smashed
in the middle of the road.

CHAPTER TEN

JANEY'S exam on Monday afternoon was even more difficult than she'd expected. She knew the material cold, but she felt as if somebody had scrambled the index in her brain. Only by sheer effort of will did she manage to pull out the necessary details and string them together to create answers, and the exercise left her with a headache.

Her friend Ellen was waiting in the hall, leaning against a bulletin board. "Mind if I walk you home?" She took one look at Janey's face and sympathized. "Tough test, I see. Well, it's over now, so you can relax."

Except there was a worst test yet to come, Janey thought as they left the building and waited at the stoplight. She had to go back to work today, and that meant facing Webb and hearing him out. Her only hope was that his anger had dissipated overnight—that perhaps, with a little time to reflect, he might even have seen why she'd acted as she had.

But don't count on it, she told herself philosophically.

"So tell me all about it," Ellen said. "You said you would after the holiday, you know."

Janey barely remembered making that lighthearted promise, when Ellen had spotted the diamond ring.

The ring... She'd put it on carelessly and worn it for only a matter of days, but now that she'd given it back, her finger felt naked without it.

She tried to dodge the question. "I said if it was still current news I'd tell you."

"So? My parents saw you out for dinner Saturday night

with a gorgeous man and looking like a million dollars. That's current enough for me. So what's the deal?''

They turned the corner toward Janey's apartment and found the narrow street almost blocked by a slow-moving florist's van. The driver's window was down and the young man behind the wheel was squinting at house numbers. He braked and called, ''Excuse me, can you help me find an address? The card says it's on Wilson Court, but—''

''That's what looks like an alley,'' Janey said. ''The sign fell down long ago.'' Her heart had speeded up. Her apartment was on Wilson Court.

So are several others, she reminded herself. *And you're not expecting flowers.*

''Thanks.'' The driver grinned. ''I've been on the route a year, but I've never had a delivery right around here.''

''It's not a big fresh-flower neighborhood,'' Janey agreed.

''Well, now it is.'' The driver shut off the van and walked around to the back to take out a plastic-wrapped bundle which filled both his arms. He looked at the card. ''Any idea where I'll find Janey Griffin?''

''Right here,'' Ellen said cheerfully, and pointed.

Janey's stomach dropped to her toes. Was it possible Webb had sent her flowers? And if so, were they an apology for being angry at her when all she'd done was tell the truth? A gesture of appreciation—assuming Camilla had agreed to leave him alone? A silent goodbye?

Or…was it possible he regretted letting her go yesterday?

She wouldn't even let herself carry the thought any further. Allowing herself to dream that Webb might care for her even a fraction as much as she cared for him would be as risky as spending the lottery jackpot before buying a ticket—and the repercussions would be even more severe.

More likely the flowers are from Camilla, she told herself blightingly, *to say good riddance.*

"Janey, take the flowers," Ellen ordered. "The poor man's standing there looking like he's burst into bloom." She held out a hand for Janey's backpack.

Janey gathered up the armload, holding it as tenderly as she would a sleeping Maddy. Through the plastic she could see several roses, some daisies and mums, even a couple of tulips and several other flowers she couldn't quite place.

The driver climbed back into the van, and Ellen almost dragged Janey down the narrow driveway to the apartment door.

"And you were going to try to convince me it was over, weren't you?" Ellen chided. "Come on, get the flowers inside before they freeze. Do you have any idea how expensive tulips *are* out of season?"

Janey set the bundle on the kitchen counter and pulled off the tiny envelope, which had been stapled to the plastic. The card inside was typed. She tried to take a deep breath before she read it, but her throat was so tight she couldn't.

"With our apologies for misjudging you," it said. "Roger and Marilyn Herrington."

The fragment of hope, which had survived despite all her efforts to be realistic, drained out of her body, leaving her feeling as limp as a cooked noodle.

Ellen was unabashedly looking over her shoulder at the card. Janey handed it to her. "I've got to get ready for work. If you want to arrange the flowers, help yourself."

"And if I don't, what are you going to do? Leave them lying here to wilt? It's not their fault—whatever you're mad about."

True enough, Janey thought. Even if this apology wasn't from the person she'd hoped for, it was pleasant to know that the Herringtons at least had appreciated her honesty and regretted their haste. It didn't exactly mean they'd be inviting her to their next dinner party, of course; a dignified and restrained apology for misjudging her was hardly the same thing as taking her to their hearts. But the gesture helped to restore her confidence that she had done the right thing—taken the only action possible.

She hoped Webb had cooled off enough to realize that, too. If he hadn't, the little talk they were due to have would be almighty unpleasant.

At least it would be the last little talk they'd ever have, though the thought was no comfort at all to Janey.

The factory was noisy, busy and brilliantly lit; from the bustle, an observer wouldn't guess that the line had been closed down for days, silent till just a few hours before.

Janey came on the floor at four o'clock, blinking at the too-bright light, recoiling from the too-loud noise. How quickly she had gotten used to the idea of leaving all this behind. And how much more quickly she was going to have to get over that notion, because after her actions yesterday there would be no loan from Webb, no escape from the factory. She'd simply have to make the best of it. Sooner or later the talk about her and the boss would die down—if she was lucky.

Her supervisor nodded curtly and waved her toward her usual machine. Janey was startled; she'd fully expected a message telling her to report to Webb's office immediately.

Perhaps, she thought, he *had* cooled off, and he'd decided to let things stand as they were. There was no way to turn back the clock or credibly deny what she'd said. The damage she'd done couldn't be repaired, and whatever Webb thought, Janey still believed that any damage she'd inflicted had been offset by good.

What else did they need to talk about, after all? He already had his ring back, so he didn't need to call her in to demand its return. And it was darned sure he wasn't going to summon her to his office to chat about designing his new factory...

She had to bite her lip hard to keep the tears back. Only now, when it was too late, could she admit even to herself how much she had wanted that job! But she hadn't longed for it only because of the career boost it would have provided for her. The main attraction—one she hadn't even recognized when they'd talked about the new factory—was that they'd be working together for another few months. And as client and architect, rather than boss and worker, there would have been more of the give-and-take she'd come to love so much. They would have once more shared their dreams...and even though it wouldn't have been the personal relationship Janey longed for, it would have been something for her to treasure forever.

But that opportunity, too, was gone.

It was almost time for the supper break before the man at the next machine started in on the suggestive remarks once more. Janey ignored him for a while, until he asked what she intended to do on her half-hour break.

She didn't look up from the machine. "I have plans."

She couldn't see his grin, but it was apparent from the way he spoke. "Doing what? Giving the boss a little... special attention?" The tone of his voice made the suggestion sound filthy.

Behind Janey's back, Webb said calmly, "Sure you wouldn't like to rephrase that?"

The worker wheeled around and stammered, "Uh... I didn't mean anything by it. Just teasing. You know—treating her like one of the guys."

Janey rolled her eyes.

"You seem a little doubtful about his sincerity, Janey," Webb observed. "How long has this been going on?"

"Since the first day I worked here. Why do you think I was so anxious to get away from the line?"

A worker on the other side snickered. "Anxious enough to…" he'd said before he thought better of it and stopped.

Webb's gaze rested thoughtfully on him till he seemed to shrivel into the concrete floor. "That's one positive point, at least," he said finally. "You obviously know you're being offensive. Both of you men will report to my office at the start of your shift tomorrow, along with your supervisor, and we'll get to the bottom of this. Janey, if you'll come with me now and make a full report…"

Twin looks of venom followed her to the door. As soon as they were in the corridor, out of sight of the factory, Janey pulled off her goggles and ear protection and faced Webb. "Talk about making my position impossible," she fumed.

"Dammit, Janey, why didn't you report this?" He didn't stop walking, and she had to lengthen her stride to keep up with him.

"Report *what?* If you hadn't heard it yourself tonight, if you'd just been told the words, wouldn't you have thought I was being a little too sensitive? And if you didn't know me, you'd no doubt have wondered if I'd been asking for that kind of treatment. Besides, what are you going to do about it? Stand behind me through every shift so they don't dare say a word?"

"There are plenty of things I can do, starting with firing those two jerks."

"Gee, won't *that* make me popular with my co-workers!"

Webb planted both hands on his hips. "So what do you want me to do?"

Suddenly all her anger was gone and only tiredness remained. "I don't know. That must be why you're the boss and I'm not. So, since you obviously weren't intending to have *this* conversation when you came out to the floor, what did you want to talk to me about?"

He didn't answer, just kept walking. The executive wing was quiet and almost dark, except for the pool of light from the open door of Webb's office. He closed the door behind them.

The quiet click of the latch might as well have been a prison lock slamming home; the effect on Janey was the same. She settled onto the edge of the silk-upholstered chair he indicated and said, trying to sound perfectly at ease, "I expected you'd have gone home by now."

"So you thought you were safe?" He sat down across from her. "I had some major things to deal with today— and unlike you, they couldn't wait."

That put her precisely in her place. "Mrs. Wilson and the Herringtons? You didn't file charges, did you?"

"What possible charges are there? It's like your problem with the smart mouths out on the line—knowing what's going on is one thing, but proving it's another. All Mrs. Wilson did was take Maddy down the sidewalk to see her grandparents. And as for Roger and Marilyn—"

"You know," Janey said thoughtfully, "it was pretty stupid of them to come to the house anyway, where they could so easily be seen and recognized. If they'd met Mrs. Wilson in the park, they could have been gone with Maddy before anybody knew what had happened. You don't suppose they *wanted* to be caught?"

"I'm not about to explore the workings of their minds. I know, however, that they got a good lecture from their attorney today, and I don't believe there will be any problem in the future."

"I still think they meant well, and they'll always be Maddy's grandparents, no matter what. What about Mrs. Wilson?"

"As long as she doesn't ask me for a reference, I'm willing to live and let live."

"But she's gone?" She didn't need an answer. "Then I'm surprised you're still here and not at home with Maddy. So let's make this fast, shall we? I'm sorry, Webb."

"You must be joking. You can't mean you actually regret not keeping your mouth shut."

"No," Janey said levelly. "I'm sorry that my telling the truth ended up blowing your plan, but I don't regret doing it. All I could see right then was the danger Maddy was in, and her safety was suddenly more important than anything else."

"I know. That was apparent."

He didn't even sound angry anymore, just weary. For an instant she wondered why he'd bothered to seek her out, and then she remembered the money that had been part of the deal—the considerable sum she'd bargained for, which of course he had no intention of paying out now.

"It's the money, isn't it?" she said. "Don't worry about it. I don't expect you to follow through on your end of the bargain since I didn't complete mine." She pushed herself up from the chair. "There are no hard feelings on my part. I hope you don't have any lasting ones for me, either." She held out a hand.

He ignored it. "You'll still need money."

The flat statement brought the prickle of tears. She hadn't expected that he'd give her needs a thought. "I have a job." She tried to put a note of humor into her voice, to help fight off the tears. "Unless you don't want to see me around at all?"

He stood up then, but only to walk over to his desk and

reach into the shallow middle drawer. "Here, take this. I don't have any use for it." He held out a black velvet box with a gesture that Janey found eerily familiar. "You can sell the ring and use the money." He dropped it into her hand as if the velvet was furnace-hot.

How eager he was to get rid of it, to put behind him the memories the diamond represented—the memories of her. The thought made Janey irrationally angry. "And how, exactly, am I supposed to do that? I don't know a single jeweler, and whatever you think, I'm not familiar enough with pawnshops that I can come in off the street and get cash for a ten-thousand-dollar diamond ring with no questions asked."

"Twenty-five thousand," he said.

She looked at the box, and then at him, with horror. She'd been walking around Chicago wearing a ring worth... "Oh, that really helps me feel better," she said with heavy irony.

"It won't pay for an elegant life-style, but—"

"I'm not used to an elegant life-style. Wasn't that the whole point in the beginning?" She turned the box over in her hand, letting the velvet tickle her palm.

She struggled against the desire to say thank-you and put the box in her pocket and walk away. Not because of the ring's value, for she would never, never sell it, but because of the very memories he wanted to dispel. The same memories, for her, were pleasant ones—of washing dishes, and playing with Maddy in the park, and talking of new factories.

If the ring had meant anything to him, if it had been truly a gift and not just a way to get rid of an unpleasant reminder, she would have taken it. Instead, she put the box back in his hand. "No, thanks, Webb. Keep the ring—

because you do have a use for it, as a reminder not to get yourself into any more stupid scams.''

''Funny,'' he said wryly. ''That's just about what Gran said.''

He didn't offer any further explanation; he seemed to be sunk in his own thoughts, staring down at the velvet box.

He's no doubt thinking it's a bad penny coming back to taunt him, Janey reflected.

There was nothing more to say, no reason for her to remain. But it took the greatest effort of Janey's life to pull herself away from him, knowing that she would never again see him like this but only from the distance, and only as a boss.

She knew she would long for those glimpses, however rare, and treasure them. She knew she would love him regardless.

She was almost to the door when he spoke, so softly that she wasn't sure she heard him right. ''Maddy cried for you this morning.''

Her heart rolled itself into a knot. ''I'm sorry. I never meant to let her—''

''I know you didn't. Nevertheless...''

''I don't suppose... I mean, if you think it would help, Webb, I'll go see her. But it would probably only make things worse.''

''I'm sure it would. Make things worse, I mean. Unless...''

She waited till the tension drew her nerves out like taffy. ''Unless what?''

''You're very fond of her, aren't you?''

''Stupid question. Can anyone not love Maddy?''

''Not everybody would have torpedoed a sweet deal like you had going for you—several years of tuition and living expenses and a nice little commission for a factory just waiting for you to graduate—because they were concerned for the well-being of a year-old child. All you had to do was keep quiet."

"Don't remind me." Janey tried to keep her voice light.

"It's too late to go back now, of course. But you still need the money. So I was thinking—"

"Not *again*. Honestly, Webb, how you can stand there with that ring in your hand and plan another scam—"

"It's not a scam, Janey. It's a straightforward deal."

Her instinct for self-preservation told her to throw the nearest heavy object at him and run while she could. But something about his voice kept her nailed to the spot.

"You can have it all, Janey. All the money you need to finish school, with no question about paying it back."

"What's the price?" She managed, she thought, to sound as if she was barely interested.

"Me," he said flatly. "A marriage of convenience."

Janey's ears filled with a steady roar that was worse than the factory floor on a busy night. In the space of a few seconds he had offered her the world and then snatched it away again. She could have the man she loved...but she would always know that his heart still belonged to Sibyl. She could be his wife...but only in name.

"I learned this week that Gran's right about one thing at least—Maddy not only needs a mother, but she longs for one. She doesn't even know what she's missing, but she wants it anyway. She's formed a great attachment for you, and you're very fond of her. So..."

She could be the mother of his child...but she would never carry his baby under her heart.

She snapped her fingers. "So just like that, you're ready to give up your determination to stay single."

Webb shrugged. "We got along all right, I thought. It's not like we'd be living in each others' pockets."

And that, Janey thought, was the crux of the problem, wasn't it? "Wait a minute. You're the one who suggested we have an affair. Why are you suddenly sounding like the spokesman for celibacy?"

"I didn't say we couldn't have fun in bed together. I said we didn't have to." She was still chewing on that one when he went on softly, "I'm not asking you to give up your career, either. Maddy needs a mother, but it doesn't have to be one who's with her every instant. You could have your independent practice, Janey—the one it would take years to build otherwise. With that, you'd have time for Maddy—because you could accept only the work you like, and take or turn down any commission without thinking about the money."

This is absolutely not sporting of him, she told herself. He was offering her the universe...except for the corner of it that mattered most.

"Love isn't the only thing to build a marriage on," Webb said.

"Neither is sex, but they'd both better be considered ahead of time, or the road's going to be awfully rocky." She took a deep breath. Her body screamed *yes*. Her brain, still coolly logical, said *no*.

How could she bring herself to refuse something she wanted so badly? But how could she enter into an agreement that included so much—and yet so little?

There was only one possibility: she was going to have to turn him down, and she couldn't even tell him why, for she couldn't stand to have him look at her in pity, or—perhaps even worse—not understand why loving him should enter into her decision at all.

"I married a woman who didn't love me once. Why not again?"

"Sibyl?" Her voice was no more than a startled squeak.

"But that's impossible. How could any woman—" She broke off, horrified at what she had almost said.

"And what the hell would you know about it?"

Janey swallowed hard. He hadn't said he didn't love Sibyl, she reminded herself. He'd said Sibyl hadn't loved him. The difference was as wide as the Pacific.

His voice was gruff. "What did you mean, Janey? *How could any woman...* what?"

She was in for it now; once he had his teeth into a subject, dynamite wouldn't blast him loose. And perhaps, Janey thought, it would be just as well if she told him how she felt. The damage to her pride was done already; she wouldn't like seeing pity in his eyes, but it couldn't possibly make her feel any worse.

And the benefit was that once he knew she'd fallen in love with him, that would be the end of it. He wouldn't annoy her any further with propositions, or deals, or offers of a marriage of convenience; he'd be too busy running in the opposite direction.

When a man didn't want to be married at all, he might bring himself to contract some cool alliance. But to have a wife who was in love with him, who might actually want his attention, who might court him, who might attempt to awaken his love in return... To such a man, that prospect would be the worst imaginable.

And just to be assured that she wouldn't have to face this question again made a little self-humiliation bearable.

Janey took a deep breath and squared her shoulders, but she couldn't quite make her gaze meet his. "I was going to say, *How could any woman not love you the way I do?*"

She knew from the silence in the room what she would see in his face, and it took only a glance to confirm it. Webb was stunned; he looked as if he was still standing only because he'd forgotten how to sit down.

Janey tried to keep her voice from shaking but didn't quite succeed. "Well, I'm sure that leaves us nothing else to say to each other. So I'll get out of here and let you—"

"*Don't you dare.*"

Each word was low and precise and clipped; Janey had never heard anybody sound so authoritarian, and she froze.

His footsteps were almost silent on the plush carpet. He stopped less than a foot from her. "And as for having nothing to say to each other...what about this?"

In the few seconds it had taken him to cross the room, Janey had braced herself for angry words. She'd even considered—and dismissed—the possibility that he might be shocked to the point of violence. But she hadn't anticipated that he would pull her into his arms instead, that his mouth would come down against hers—demanding, caressing, pleading, insisting—until she was incapable of breathing, much less struggling. Until all she could do was surrender to the instinctive need to respond to him, to melt into his body and kiss him back with the full force of her own longing.

By the time he raised his head she was dizzy and the air in the office looked pale orange. She couldn't quite identify the expression in his eyes. Was it triumph or sheer sensual pleasure?

He whispered, "You do love me."

"I told you that already," Janey said irritably. "And I suppose because I was crazy enough to tell you, you expect me to fall into bed with you tonight."

"Only if you insist. I'm willing to wait till you marry me."

"But I'm not *going* to marry you. That's the whole point. What you did wasn't fair. Dammit, Webb, I only told you that to explain why I won't marry you—and you used it against me—"

"That's right," he admitted. "I used it deliberately and it wasn't fair. And I'll use it again and again till I get the answer I want."

Janey shook her head. "I won't—"

"I love you, Janey."

She stared at him, and saw the truth in his eyes, and the quiver that started deep inside her spread till every cell was shivering with exultation.

"Of course Maddy needs a mother," he said. "But that's not why I asked you to marry me. That's not why I want you to have your own office and the freedom to choose the work you'll do. I just thought those things might be more tempting. And...well, I didn't really care why you accepted me, as long as you did."

"More tempting than *you?*" Janey shook her head in wonder. "Webb, I would never have believed you could have so little experience with women that you could be deluded like that."

"I have plenty of experience with females," he said. "Not a lot with women. At least, not a woman like you. That's probably why it took me so long to understand what was happening."

She didn't ask, but he obviously saw the question in her eyes.

"When you faced Roger and Marilyn yesterday," he said, "and sacrificed yourself for Maddy's good—and yet you didn't condemn them for what they'd done because you understood—that was when the light clicked on. But long before that, there were little things...like realizing how beautiful you are. It'll take me a year to tell them all."

Janey drew a long, deep breath of sheer happiness. *A year to tell them...* And all the years that followed, as well.

"So," he said. "Are you going to marry me?"

"You're sure, Webb? You've been so dead set against the institution—"

"I don't have anything against marriage, really. I just didn't trust my judgment, after Sibyl—and I was damned sure I couldn't live through another mistake on that scale."

She waited, almost holding her breath.

"I thought she loved me. I didn't realize that she was so entirely self-centered she couldn't love anyone else, not till it was too late—Maddy was on the way. That was actually when I found out what Sibyl was really like. She'd told me she was anxious to have children, but in fact she was taking the pill. I didn't know it until she discovered it had failed. She was horrified, too hysterical to keep quiet—which was fortunate, I think, or else she probably would never have let me find out. She'd have just quietly…dealt with it."

"Oh, no." Janey's voice was no more than a breath.

"By the time she realized what was going on, the pregnancy was pretty far along, and I issued a few threats of what I'd do if she arranged for anything to happen to that child."

"The television set?" At his look of bewilderment, Janey said, "The broken one in the master bedroom. Is that when—"

"Oh, no. If I'd done that, she'd have had a new one the next day. She broke it herself, the night she died." He paused and said deliberately, "Right after I asked her why, if she was so miserable with me, she didn't just drive into a bridge."

"And so she did. Oh, Webb—"

He shook his head. "There was ice that night, and she always drove too fast. I've never thought it was truly deliberate, because she was too self-centered to destroy herself. If she'd managed to take Maddy with her that night, though—"

"She tried?"

"It was Mrs. Wilson's night off—which was part of the argument. Sibyl wanted a second baby nurse because she said I paid more attention to Maddy than to her. I suppose it was true—at least Maddy smiled at me now and then. I said no, Sibyl grabbed up the baby, I snatched Maddy from her arms, and she smashed the television controls and stormed out. That was the last time I saw her. They called me after the crash, but she was gone by the time I got to the hospital."

Janey reached up to stroke his cheek, trying to give him some of her own strength.

"I passed the wreck site on the way home. The baby seat was still strapped in the back of the car—at least, there were shreds of it. If I hadn't grabbed her, Maddy would be gone, too."

Janey hugged him tightly. "No wonder you weren't in any hurry to find her a stepmother! But your grandmother, Webb—why didn't she understand?"

"Gran doesn't know any of this, Janey, so if you don't mind—"

"It's not my place to tell her." Janey had her doubts, though. That crack of Camilla's about not even trying to imitate Sibyl had suddenly taken on another meaning. Or was she fooling herself, trying to pretend that Webb's grandmother might not be quite so opposed to her as she'd let on?

"You haven't answered the question," Webb reminded. "Marry me?"

"What about Camilla?" she said doubtfully. "If she's still so convinced we're a bad combination, I don't know if—"

"I haven't a clue what goes on in her mind, and I'm not

sure I want to. But she told me yesterday you were worth three of me any day of the week."

Janey was confused. "But yesterday as I was leaving the house, I heard her tell you..." She colored a little, embarrassed at having so casually admitted to eavesdropping, but Webb didn't seem to have noticed. "Camilla said, 'You got caught, didn't you?' She said it as if she was sad that you'd made a big mistake and had to face the consequences—"

He smiled wryly. "She meant that I'd set up this great little trap and promptly snared myself in it. I engineered a fake engagement to an obviously impossible person, who turned out not to be impossible after all—and then I fell in love with her. And—if you'll recall—when Gran said that you'd just walked out on me."

"She didn't try to stop me."

"I think she was giving us both a chance to think it over. And as for what the Herringtons think—they can go jump in Lake Michigan for all I care."

She thought about the flowers, arranged by Ellen's expert hand, which waited for her in her apartment. "It might take some time, but I think that'll be all right."

"If it takes the next fifty years, I still don't care—I'll marry whomever I please. However, when Roger came by today to apologize, he told me if I still thought you were unsuitable I ought to have my head examined. So I don't think we'll have any trouble there, either. Will you at least answer the question, Janey?"

"About marrying you?" She wrinkled her forehead thoughtfully. "Didn't I tell you once that if I changed my mind about it you'd be the first to find out?"

"Yes, you did. And...?"

She darted a mischievous look at him. "I'll let you know when I decide."

Once more, he kissed her into oblivion, and when she got her breath back, she said, "All right, I give up—I'll marry you. Not that I'm objecting to that sort of treatment, exactly, but my fingers are starting to turn blue from lack of oxygen."

"Good. Now that little matter's settled, you're quitting your job tonight, too."

"Being a bit dictatorial all the way around, aren't you?"

"We both have better things to do at midnight than meet in Copeland Products' parking lot."

"If you insist. As long as we're speaking of the factory, Webb—you said something a while ago about the new one just waiting for me to graduate. You mean you've already made up your mind it's mine?"

"Not quite. If you asked me right now to give you the job, I'd say no, but not for the reason you think."

She frowned. "You're not making much sense, you know."

"Because if I guaranteed it to you, you'd always wonder if you were really the best. So you'll have to compete, but I'll be very disappointed if you don't win in a walk. But I'd much rather not talk about production lines tonight." He pushed her hair back where it had come loose from the braid so he could nibble at her neck. "That *is* going to be an interesting scar," he murmured. "The spot where that chunk of hot metal landed and started off this whole thing."

"Maybe you shouldn't fire the jerk at the next machine, since it was what he said that made me slip. No, wait— that was a different jerk. This one you can fire."

"Thanks for giving me permission to run my business," Webb said dryly. "Wedding at Christmas, when you're between semesters?"

"I think that could be arranged." But suddenly the enormity of it all overwhelmed her. She'd walked into this office an hour ago expecting never to speak to him again afterward, and now... "You're sure, Webb? It's all happened so suddenly—"

"I'm sure," he said. "I knew it from the beginning, really. I remember thinking almost as soon as I saw you that you were perfect. Utterly and absolutely perfect."

"For scamming your grandmother, you mean."

"Yes, but also for me, even if I wasn't smart enough to see it right away. For always."

He pulled her close once more, and Janey's last niggle of doubt faded away.

Neither of them heard the office door open. And they probably wouldn't have seen the two people standing there, either, if Maddy—bundled up in her great-grandmother's arms—hadn't spotted Janey and yelled with all the power she could muster, "Mama!"

They jerked apart and turned to face Camilla. She looked at them soberly for a long moment, and then she said quietly, "Now isn't that nice? Maddy finally got it right." She handed the baby over, and smiled radiantly as Webb drew Janey close once more—with their daughter in her arms.

If you enjoyed what you just read,
then we've got an offer you can't resist!

Take 2 bestselling
love stories FREE!

Plus get a FREE surprise gift!

 **HARLEQUIN®**
Makes any time special ™

WIN A DREAM

In celebration of Harlequin®'s golden anniversary

Enter to win a *dream!* You could win:

- A luxurious trip for two to **The Renaissance Cottonwoods Resort** in Scottsdale, Arizona, or

- A bouquet of flowers once a week for a year from **FTD**, or

- A $500 shopping spree, or

- A fabulous bath & body gift basket, including **K-tel's** *Candlelight and Romance* 5-CD set.

Look for **WIN A DREAM** flash on specially marked Harlequin® titles by Penny Jordan, Dallas Schulze, Anne Stuart and Kristine Rolofson in October 1999*.

FTD

RENAISSANCE. COTTONWOODS RESORT
SCOTTSDALE, ARIZONA

K·TEL

*No purchase necessary—for contest details send a self-addressed envelope to Harlequin Makes Any Time Special Contest, P.O. Box 9069, Buffalo, NY, 14269-9069 (include contest name on self-addressed envelope). Contest ends December 31, 1999. Open to U.S. and Canadian residents who are 18 or over. Void where prohibited.

PHMATS-GR

Harlequin Romance®

Coming Next Month

#3575 BRIDEGROOM ON APPROVAL Day Leclaire

Hanna went to the Cinderella Ball intending to bring home a husband—on a trial-only basis! Marco Salvatore wasn't looking for a bride, yet he wanted Hanna the moment he saw her. They were married by midnight...but could this marriage last a lifetime?

Fairytale Weddings: *The Fairytale Weddings Ball: come single, leave wed!*

#3576 ONE MOTHER WANTED Jeanne Allan

Zane Peters, the man Allie once loved—still loves—needs a wife if he is to keep custody of his motherless little girl. Allie offers to marry him for his daughter's sake. But can she ever become his wife for real?

Hope Valley Brides: *Four weddings, one Colorado family*

#3577 AN INNOCENT BRIDE Betty Neels

Aunt Thirza's death had left Katrina with a small cottage—and, though she didn't know it, Simon Glenville, the wonderful doctor who had cared for her aunt. He knew he loved Katrina, and when the time was right he would propose....

White Weddings: *True love is worth waiting for....*

#3578 OUTBACK WIFE AND MOTHER Barbara Hannay

Fletcher Hardy was adamant that his cattle station was no place for a city-girl like Ally. Until she turned up at Wallaroo as his four-year-old godson's new nanny, intending to prove she could survive the Outback—and be the perfect wife and mother!

Daddy Boom: *Who says bachelors and babies don't mix?*